The Black Vaults Experiment

Also by Patrick C. Walsh

Stories of the supernatural

13 Ghosts of Winter

The Mac Maguire detective mysteries

The Body in the Boot

The Dead Squirrel

The Weeping Women

The Blackness

23 Cold Cases

Two Dogs

All available in Amazon Books

Patrick C. Walsh

The Black Vaults Experiment

The first of the 'Ghost Field' series

Garden City Ink

A Garden City Ink ebook
www.gardencityink.com

First published in Great Britain in 2018
All rights reserved
Copyright © 2018 Patrick C Walsh

The right of Patrick C. Walsh to be identified as the author of this work has been asserted in accordance with Section 77 of the Copyright, Designs and Patents Act 1988.

No part of this publication may be reproduced, stored in a retrieval system, or transmitted, in any form or means, electronic, mechanical, photocopying, recording or otherwise, without the prior permission of the copyright holder.

All characters in this publication are fictitious and any resemblance to real persons, living or dead, is purely co-incidental.

Cover art © Patrick C Walsh 2018
Garden City Ink Design

*"Now I know what a ghost is.
Unfinished business, that's what."*

Salman Rushdie, The Satanic Verses

For Montague, Edgar, Ambrose, Herbert and Howard without whom this book could not have been written

Before...

The team started work on the second floor of the old pub, ripping out all the old fittings and getting down to the bare walls and floor joists. They were getting on with it as fast as possible for there was a deadline to meet and a big bonus riding on it for all of them. The builders were mostly Irish, Polish and Romanian, strong men who worked hard and drank hard and who were afraid of nothing.

Nothing except for the room on the first floor that is.

None of the men wanted to work in there for some reason and so the foreman, Pat Whelan, had decided to keep them working on the second floor while he figured out what to do about it. They'd told him stories about seeing things in there, strange things that had scared them. One of his best men had walked off the site yesterday vowing that he'd never set foot in the place again. They were falling behind time and he knew he'd have problems if he didn't nip this in the bud.

The big problem for Pat was that he believed them. They were a tight team and he'd known most of them for some years. He also knew that they weren't the type of men who scared easily if at all. He sighed as he reluctantly concluded that he'd just have to investigate it for himself. He wasn't looking forward to it.

Pat was a giant of a man from Dublin who could walk into any pub in London without fear yet, as he and his friend Nico walked into the large open space on the first floor, he felt the hairs on the back of his neck stand up and his stomach turn to water. There was something else in the room with them, of that Pat was sure.

It was late in the day and most of the huge room was in shadow. He pulled the switch to turn on the lights but nothing happened.

'Bloody fuse blown again,' Nico said.

There was light enough to see anyway. The foreman peered towards the far end of the room and started inching his way forward. He could see something but it was indistinct at first. Just random dots of light like fireflies in the air. They slowly walked towards it. As they neared the far end of the room it suddenly turned cold, a bitter chilling cold that was unexpected. Pat could see his breath turn an icy white in front of him. He slowly moved his hand forward and then pulled it quickly back.

'What is it Pat?' Nico asked in a frightened whisper.

'Cold, it's not a draught though, it's more like the inside of a freezer,' Pat replied in a low voice.

Nico could hear the fear in his friend's voice and somehow it made him feel a little better. If Pat was scared then it was okay for him to be scared too.

The fireflies now surrounded them, intense points of radiant blue light that flew in a spiral at ever increasing speeds. Looking at them made both Pat and Nico feel a little dizzy. Then they felt a sort of expectant prickling inside their skulls. Something was going to happen.

The dots of light slowly coalesced into a ball of white light. It slowly came into focus and finally Pat could see it.

It was a coffin. It stood right in front of him with her dead in it. He was a boy of five or six again, forced to kiss the lips of a dead grandmother by a drunk and overbearing father. She lay still, small and pale and wrinkled, with her eyes shut. Her hands were crossed over her chest and they rested on a black bible. He pulled back, scared of the dead thing beneath him. He didn't want to kiss her. He was afraid that he'd wake her up and then those dead eyes would open and take him with her into the darkness. He heard his father curse loudly and felt the power of his huge hand on the back of his small head. He pushed his head down, down towards her face, towards the frozen mask of death. She smelt of piss and chemicals.

The dead lips were cold and clammy and he pulled his head away as soon as he could but it was too late! The eyelids opened and her black malevolent eyes saw him. A bony hand reached out of the coffin and clawed at him, trying to pull him down with her into the world of the dead. He screamed in terror. He felt as if he was about to fall into the coffin and eternal darkness when he felt hands pulling him back.

Somehow Nico got himself and his boss out of the room. They looked at each other as they stood on the landing and then they both thundered down the stairs and ran straight out of the building. Pat looked around and was quite stunned to see normality all around him. People were walking by, buses and cars were driving slowly past and everything was as usual. He looked down at his feet and at the solid pavement below them. He felt as if he couldn't even trust that now. As normal as things looked the sense of that other world still hung about him.

He shook his head to try and clear it and then turned to his friend.

'Fuck me, Nico did you see that?' he asked.

Nico was white faced and his hands were shaking.

'I did and I wish I didn't.'

Pat knew what he meant and he too wished that it might be possible to un-see things. However the vision was burnt into his mind and he knew it wasn't going to go away anytime soon. He suddenly felt nauseous so he bent over and threw up into the gutter. He spat the last of it out and wiped his lips on the back of his hand.

He turned and looked up at the building. It looked back down on him and he felt that he could sense its dark and evil presence. He knew he had to get his men out of there and the sooner the better. He moved towards the doorway and then stopped. His feet refused to cross the threshold and he knew he'd never be able to set foot inside the pub ever again. He heard a noise and looked up. A wind had started blowing and the aged and fading pub sign was squeaking as the air moved it to and fro. Pat thought it had been aptly named.

The Black Vaults.

Chapter One – A Fry Up

'Are you sure about this?' the professor's wife asked as she watched him eat the fry-up she'd cooked him for breakfast.

He was going to be away for a few days and she wanted to make sure he had some proper food in him before he went.

'Liz you worry too much,' he replied.

'Well it doesn't even strike me as being very ethical. It's a wonder that the university gave it the green light,' she said giving him a long hard look.

Her husband's sheepish expression told her all she needed to know.

'Oh God, you didn't tell them did you? I'll bet there's not a word about this in the research protocol is there?'

'Well not exactly, I kind of fudged it a bit here and there I suppose if I'm honest,' he said before despatching a forkful of pork sausage.

She gave him a mournful look and shook her head.

'You'll go too far one of these days Martin, you really will.'

'Oh come on, you've got to admit that I've done okay so far, Professor of Anomalistic Psychology at the age of thirty nine, youngest one in the country too.'

'Anomalistic Psychology, God the names you people make up for things.'

'Well we couldn't call it Paranormal Studies now could we? People might think we believed in that claptrap,' he said disdainfully as he wiped the plate clean with a piece of toast.

'So where's it all happening then? A suitably spooky location I hope,' she said as she picked up his empty plate.

'The Black Vaults,' he said in a hammy horror accent.

'Well that doesn't exactly sound like a barrel of laughs. What is it?'

'It's a pub,' he shouted at her as she walked towards the kitchen. 'The Black Vaults, Frognall. Not far off the Finchley Road.'

Liz poked her head back into the dining room.

'Your experiment is in a pub in North London? That's not exactly Transylvania either is it?'

'Oh people see lots of ghosts in pubs and they always believe it too. The fact that most of them were blind drunk at the time never seems to make any difference.'

Liz came back in and sat down.

'What's so special about this pub then?' she asked.

'Well it's old, nearly a hundred and sixty years old in fact. The first owner was a man called Black hence the name. It's one of those massive early Victorian pubs that were built on three floors, the bar downstairs, the function room over that and then the living quarters at the top, so there'll be lots of ground for us to cover.'

'You didn't answer my question,' she said tartly.

'Okay the previous owners had left the place lying idle for more than twenty years, no one knows why as it's certainly in a prime area for real estate. There was also a strange recommendation in the will advising the new owners of the pub to knock it down. The new owners didn't. Instead they sold it to a pub chain for a massive amount of money and they're currently in the process of renovating it. I believe that it's going to be called 'The Frog and All' probably because it's near Frognall I suppose. Not very original but there you go.'

He stopped and looked at his wife.

'And?' she prompted.

He sighed. He knew that she'd winkle it out of him eventually so he decided he might as well come clean with her.

'Well the workmen who were doing the renovations pulled out last week. They said that several of their men had been scared shitless, their words, by the place and they refused to carry on working until something was done about it.'

'Ah now we're getting to it. So the pub chain thought that they'd bring in the famous Professor of Anomalistic Psychology who would then solve all their problems. Wouldn't a priest have been a better option?'

Martin cleared his throat.

'They tried that first but it didn't work out too well.'

'So what happened then?'

'He ran out screaming.'

She looked at her husband with some concern.

'Just watch out that you're not biting off more than you can chew. I take it that Jerzy's going with you?'

Jerzy was his graduate research assistant. He was paid peanuts but he loved the work. He was indispensable to Martin as he was the one who set up all the technical equipment and sensors and actually knew how it all worked. He was also a great believer in Martin's theories and Martin loved him for that too.

'Of course, I couldn't do anything without Jerzy.'

'Well thank God that there'll be at least one sensible person there. Who are the lab rats?'

'Now that's a bit unfair, they're not lab rats they're psychology students. If you must know Jerzy told me that they're all chomping at the bit for the experiment to start,' Martin protested.

'That's because they think they're going ghost hunting,' she said. 'They don't know that it's really them that you'll be observing.'

'Don't worry nothing's going to happen to them or anyone else. It will hopefully be an interesting experience that will go some way towards confirming my theories and then I'll be back before you know it.'

'Where are you staying?'

'There's a place just around the corner from the pub, one of those budget chain hotels. I've been and had a look, it's cheap but it's not bad.

I've booked us all in for three nights.' Seeing the concerned look on his wife's face Martin added, 'It'll be fine Liz, don't worry.'

His wife gave him a look that told him that she was far from convinced about the whole thing.

'Just watch yourself and keep your hotel door locked when you go to sleep.'

Martin laughed out loud.

'Why? Do you think that the ghosts are going to follow me back to the hotel or something?'

'No Jerzy told me that two of your volunteers are girls and you know all too well how attractive students can find their professors, even if they are just broken down old hacks like you.'

'Well thanks for that. Anyway I'm all too aware of the dangers of getting romantically involved with students after what happened to Barry Walker. I promise that I'll be good and keep my pecker firmly in my pocket.'

Martin hoped that this would make Liz smile but it didn't.

'Just make sure you do and look after yourself. Remember to eat regularly and make sure that Jerzy doesn't eat too much crap either, you know what he's like.'

She kissed him and stood watching him through the window as he drove off. She hoped that she'd managed to keep herself from looking too worried about her husband's latest experiment but worried she was. For some reason she had the bleak feeling that no good would come of it.

Chapter Two – The Black Vaults

Martin thought about what the night might bring as he drove into London. He'd had some theories for a while now but they had stayed just that as he'd never been able to prove them one way or the other. He'd begun to have some doubts lately and he was desperately hoping that this might be the experiment that would finally prove he was on the right track after all.

Or not, he thought, reminding himself that it was also quite probable that the experiment might blow his theories to smithereens and that he should prepare himself for that eventuality too.

He went to the hotel first and checked himself in. He threw his bag into his room, which was both cleaner and bigger than he'd expected, had a quick wash and then headed straight for the pub which was just around the corner.

He felt a little shiver of excitement as the pub came into view. He looked at his watch and realised that he was early. He'd have to wait outside for a while until the contractor's representative turned up with the keys. He stepped back and looked at the outside of the building. It stood solidly on a corner and it was three stories high. From the outside the brickwork seemed in good condition as did the ornately carved stone lintels above the windows. Most of the original sash windows seemed to have survived on the first and second floors too. The windows on the ground floor were blocked off by thick plate steel shutters and the door was covered by a massive sheet of plate steel held in place by a substantial padlock. The pub name above the window had been hastily painted over with black paint.

They'd left the pub sign up though. It didn't have the usual charming picture on it that most London pubs seemed to favour these days. Instead it consisted of a jet black background with the words 'The Black Vaults' picked out in a now faded gold coloured script. While he waited he thought of what a suitable picture might be for a pub with such a name but he couldn't come up with anything.

'Are you the professor then?' a deep Irish voice said with some scepticism.

'Pat?' Martin asked as he turned around.

All Martin knew was that the representative's name was Pat Whelan and that he'd been the foreman on the renovation project. Pat was Irish and he looked it. He was in his thirties, ginger bearded, well over six feet tall and as broad as a barn. He looked Martin up and down in some disbelief.

Martin was casually dressed in blue jeans and a bright red hoodie with the cover of an old Pink Floyd album emblazoned across the front. He was used to such disbelief as he knew he looked a lot younger than his thirty nine years.

Looking younger had been the bane of his life when he'd been growing up. He'd only been able to stop taking an ID with him when he went for a drink after he'd turned twenty five. He was getting to an age now when he was quite glad of it though.

'Martin Jorgensen,' Martin said as he offered his hand to the big Irishman.

Pat's huge hand engulfed his and Martin could feel the hard skin calloused by years of manual work. For a moment he feared for the state of his fingers after a handshake with such a man but Pat's grip was surprisingly soft, as though he was all too aware of his own strength.

'Are you really a professor now? You're not codding me are you?' Pat asked.

Martin wasn't sure what 'codding' meant exactly but he got the general idea from the big man's disbelieving expression.

'Yes, I'm really a professor,' he replied with some weariness and not for the first time.

He took out a card and gave it to the Irishman who looked at it for some time. He finally looked up at Martin.

'Professor of Anomalistic Psychology, now what the feck is that?' Patrick asked, his face crinkling up in puzzlement.

'Things that go bump in the night, ghosts and ghouls.'

'Well you've come to the right place for that then,' Pat said.

He looked up at the pub's exterior with a serious expression on his face.

'Take my word you'll find as many of them as you want in there.'

Pat handed Martin the keys and told him where the main power switch was and where all the power cables could be found.

'Well you can show me yourself, can't you?' Martin said as he opened the padlock that held the steel door shut. He swung the plate steel door open and behind it there was another door. It had a square glass panel in it that had 'The Black Vaults' etched on it in ornate script.

Pat shook his head and took a big step back.

'I'll not be setting a foot in there ever again if I can help it.'

'You were part of the team that was working in there, weren't you?'

'I wish I could say I wasn't but I was. It's a strange thing indeed for an Irishman to be scared of setting foot inside a pub but that's the truth of it alright.'

'So what happened in there? Did you see anything yourself?'

Martin was surprised to see a look of fear briefly cross Pat's face.

'I did but if it's all the same to you I'd prefer to forget all about it. If you'll take my advice you'll forget about having anything to do with this place too.' Pat looked up at the building again and this time his look was full of hatred. 'They should have let us tear it down brick by brick and then had us sow the land with salt. I never used to believe in the devil until I worked in there but now I do. Do you want my honest opinion?'

Martin did.

'I think you're an eejit for even wanting to set foot in there. Believe me whatever's in there is real and it's dangerous. I'll wish you good luck and you'll be needing it in there. I'll be seeing you...I hope.'

The big man looked up again at the building, crossed himself and walked off without a backward glance.

Martin thought about what the he'd said for a moment then he shrugged his shoulders, found the key for the door and went inside. Although a low winter sun shone outside it was dark inside as the light was totally blocked out by the steel shutters. A strong smell of plaster dust, mould and decay hit his nostrils. He found the main power switch just where Pat had said it would be and a line of temporary lights came on. Even though it was a crisp winter's day outside the bitterness of the cold inside surprised him.

He'd seen photographs of the downstairs bar but it was still much bigger than he'd expected. It didn't look like the builders had gotten very far with their renovations on the ground floor as the huge semi-circular bar and the shelving behind were still in place. They were suitably ghostly looking as they were covered in a thick layer of white dust. Even so he had no problem imagining the pub in its heyday, men leaning on the bar chatting and drinking beer, the air full of smoke and politics.

He noticed that an old table and an assortment of chairs had been set up in a corner next to a large industrial heater. The builders must have used this as their lunch area. He pulled the table and chairs out so they were underneath one of the lights and then pulled the heater over and switched it on. It made a soft wailing sound as it pushed warm air out. He wasn't sure how much of a difference it would make in such a large space but it was something.

A shaft of winter sunlight split the room as the front door opened.

'Boss, are you here?' a voice asked hesitantly.

Martin smiled as he saw a tall, ungainly figure come through the door. His assistant was in his early twenties and, with his long hair and full beard, he looked more like an extra in a Viking movie than anything else. Despite his rough looking appearance he was genuinely one of the brightest people Martin had ever met.

'Over here Jerzy. I'm just trying to set our office up,' Martin replied.

'I could do with a hand,' Jerzy said as he placed a brick in front of the door to hold it open.

Jerzy's white van was parked right outside. Martin helped him unload four large wheeled cases that were very like the ones that rock bands used for their equipment. Martin had never asked Jerzy where he got them from or mentioned the fact that some of the cases actually had the names of rock bands painted on them. Anyway they were great for transporting all of the technical equipment that they used for their 'ghost hunts' as Jerzy called them. Once they'd safely wheeled in all the cases Jerzy stopped and looked around.

'It wouldn't take much imagination to believe that something haunts this place. So what's the plan of action then?'

Martin looked at his watch.

'Okay, it's three o'clock now. I've asked the students to check into the hotel and then get here around six thirty or so. I'd be grateful if you could wait until then before you start setting up the equipment. They're supposed to help so they get to know what we use and how we use it.'

'I'm not letting amateurs touch my stuff!' Jerzy said indignantly.

'I wasn't expecting you to. Just let them watch you set it up and ask them to hand you some bits and pieces so they feel involved.'

'Oh, okay then,' Jerzy reluctantly conceded. 'A lot of that stuff's quite delicate you know.'

Martin couldn't blame Jerzy for his protective attitude towards his experimental equipment. The university wasn't exactly overgenerous when it came to equipment grants so Jerzy had to literally beg, steal and borrow to get what they needed. He'd actually built a lot of it himself and also did all the programming so as to save money.

'Have you checked into the hotel yet?' Martin asked.

'Yeah sure, I have to admit that it's better than I thought it would be.'

'Okay then, as we've got a bit of time, let's have a look around and see what we're up against,' Martin suggested.

'Is it all lit up like it is down here?' Jerzy asked.

'I'm not sure, it might be best to dig out a couple of torches just in case.'

Jerzy opened one of the cases and pulled out two long and very substantial steel clad torches. He handed Martin one. They were much better quality than the pathetic plastic ones they used last time and so Martin wasn't totally surprised when he read the words 'Property of the Department of Geology' printed on the side. He said nothing about this to Jerzy.

There were several doors leading out from the bar and they went through each one in turn to get an idea of the layout. After finding the kitchen and the gents and ladies toilets they found a set of stairs leading down to the cellar and another one leading to the function room upstairs.

'Let's try upstairs first,' Martin said with an expectant smile. 'That's where the contractors said that they had the most problems with the men.'

The wide staircase was well lit. It led them onto a landing that had five doors going off it before turning back on itself on its way up to the next floor. They opened each door in turn. They found the ladies toilets and then the gents. The third door opened onto a large room that had an old gas cooker in one corner, obviously another kitchen. The fourth door led them into a smaller room that still had some clothes rails and shelves in place, a cloakroom then. The last door took them into the function room.

The room was far larger than Martin had expected. It was well lit as rays from the low winter sun were streaming through the large windows on the opposite side of the room and supplementing the electric lights. It had a high ceiling and the room ran the complete length of the pub. It was really cold and Martin wondered if there was a large draught somewhere.

'It doesn't seem that spooky to me,' Jerzy said as he glanced around the room.

A second later a loud thump made them both quickly turn around. The door had shut all by itself. However no supernatural explanation was needed as they could both see that it was fitted with an old brass door closer.

Martin and Jerzy looked at each other and laughed.

'Don't speak too soon though,' Martin said with a smile. 'I've just met a six foot six tall Irishman who looks like he could dig a trench with his bare hands and he'd definitely disagree with you.'

They quickly looked around the room and Martin was surprised that it was more or less untouched. Red stuffed benches with brass studs still ran around the walls and above these ornate tiles ran in complicated patterns of black and white. There were lights on the walls that Martin reckoned might have been gas mantles originally. On the wall opposite the windows a huge tiled fireplace stood with a marble mantelpiece over it. Over that a panel of tiles bore the inscription 'The Black Vaults' in large ornate script and below that in smaller lettering 'Nigrum est cor Londiniae'.

'What's that mean?' Jerzy asked knowing that Martin had studied Latin at school.

'I think it says 'Black is the heart of London', although I'm not sure if that was exactly the message that the original proprietor was aiming at. Anyway it must have really been something in its day.'

'What do you think they got up to up here?' Jerzy asked as they looked around the room.

Jerzy found a large fan heater in the far corner of the room and turned it on. Like the one downstairs it made a low wailing sound.

'We'll have to turn that off when we're doing the sessions but we can turn it back on in between. At least the room won't be at freezing point while we're up here,' Martin said with a shiver.

'So what did they get up to in this room then?' Jerzy persisted.

'I know that there used to be lots of societies in Victorian days, the Masons and the Royal Antediluvian Order of Buffaloes for two. Anyway there were loads of others too and they covered just about any subject you could think of, after all there was no television in those days. This room would probably have been regularly used by the likes of them. I'm sure that they would have used it as a music hall, it's certainly big enough, and for plays too I should think. I don't think there were any theatres around this area when the pub was built and there used to be lots of little touring theatre companies in those days.'

'Like the one in Nicholas Nickleby?' Jerzy asked.

Martin had to think for a moment before he remembered.

'Oh yes of course, the Crummles!' he said with a smile. 'Yes I'd guess that would be exactly the type of thing they'd have here.'

'So what happened to make it haunted?'

'Jerzy it's not haunted, there's no such thing and that's one thing that we'll hopefully be confirming. However I did come across something that I thought was interesting.'

Martin went silent and Jerzy had to prompt him.

'Yes?'

'Oh sorry I was just thinking. Yes it was a story I read in an old newspaper a few weeks ago. I was going to tell you about it but it must have slipped my mind.'

Jerzy sat down on a bench and patted the space beside it.

'Well sit down and tell me now.'

Martin did as he was told.

'Okay it was in a copy of *The Star* newspaper from 1888. It was tucked away inside the paper as there was a much more sensational story on the front page, a story about someone called Jack the Ripper.'

'Really? Do you mean to say that this place might have something to do with the Whitechapel Murders?' Jerzy asked expectantly.

'No, all I said was that the two stories were in the same paper.'

'Oh,' Jerzy said, obviously disappointed.

'What I'm trying to say is that I think more might have been made of this story if it hadn't been for the Ripper being around at the same time and other things.'

'Okay so what's the story then?'

'Well the landlord of the pub at the time was a man named Oliver Gotobed and he had his own little secret society that used to regularly use this room. It was called 'The Frognall Aesthetes Society' but it would appear that the beauty that they all appreciated was feminine and of the paid variety.'

'They had prostitutes up here? Doing what?' Jerzy asked.

'According to the newspaper's sources it started innocently enough as a sort of striptease and this was what they still got up to on Monday nights but once a month on a Thursday evening it was different. The doors were always locked and it was strictly long serving members only. This carried on for at least two years until one member found God and, at the urging of his priest, reported Gotobed and his society to the police. On his information they raided this room on the night of 12th April 1888. They found a group of thirty two men including Gotobed and four young girls, the oldest of which was only thirteen.

They were all prostitutes. At the time of the raid one of the girls, aged just eleven, was found naked as were several of the men. They had obviously been indulging in some form of sex.'

'Perverted bastards!' Jerzy exclaimed with a look of disgust on his face.

'Exactly but there was worse to come. Hidden away behind a curtain they found a lead lined trunk containing several butcher's knives and cleavers. According to the former member all the men present, except for Gotobed and a few others, would indulge in sex with the young girls in turn and then lots would be drawn and one of the girls would be kept behind. The others would be sent home. Gotobed and a few others would then have sex with the remaining girl while threatening her with their knives. At the end of the sex session they would stab her to death. They'd then hack the body to pieces and stow it in the trunk for disposal later. It was all a sort of performance believe it or not.'

Jerzy screwed up his face and said something in Polish followed by 'You're kidding!'

'No I'm not. The police were a bit too early otherwise they might have caught them in the act of murder.'

'So what happened to Gotobed then?'

'He died in jail a few years afterwards but he lasted longer than the informant did. He was found hacked to death a week after the raid. I followed up on one of the reporters who initially covered the story, he later became quite a successful author and he mentioned the incident in his memoirs.'

'Who was he?'

'Sir Thomas Oliphaunt.'

Jerzy gave it some thought before saying, 'Never heard of him.'

'Me neither,' Martin said, 'but he was very popular around the turn of the century. Anyway in his memoirs he said that he wished he'd been able to follow up on the 'Frognall Frivollers' as they'd become known in the press. Gotobed was convicted of procuring girls under the age of consent for prostitution. Even so he was slightly unlucky as he got a much longer sentence than he would just three years before when the age of consent was just twelve. Strangely enough he was the only one who was prosecuted. According to Oliphaunt at least two of the other men attending were heavily involved in procuring the girls but they also happened to be very well connected. Oliphaunt was convinced that they were responsible for ensuring that the investigation ended with Gotobed alone. He himself was then ordered by his editor to drop the case and concentrate on the Whitechapel murders and again he put this down to the influence of these two men.'

'Did you ever find out who these men were?' Jerzy asked.

'No, Oliphaunt never mentioned names but they must have been quite powerful to be able to influence the police and a newspaper in the way he suggests. Anyway even years later he was convinced that the informant had been right and that murder had been committed right on this spot, perhaps many murders indeed.'

'God almighty, how many are we talking about?'

'Well Oliphaunt asked around the area and he said that at least twenty girls aged fourteen or under had disappeared in the previous few years and one procuress he talked to linked at least five of them directly to Gotobed. Anyway after the raid the pub was shut down for a few weeks and it was then sold to a new landlord. Everything seems to have been above board after that.'

Jerzy gave Martin's story some thought.

'Kind of fits in with your theory though, doesn't it? 'Emotional energy' and all that. If you're right there might have been a lot of that released right in this room.'

'Well as I say it's not really energy but I don't know what else to call it. But yes, I'd guess that murder would do the trick and there might have been quite a few of those carried out on this very spot. Anyway, let's go and see what's on the third floor.'

They had to turn their torches on when they got near the top of the stairs. They could see that a set of temporary lights had been set up but even Jerzy couldn't figure out how to get them to work. In the torch light they found themselves in a corridor that had doors leading off on either side.

'I guess that this is where the landlord used to live,' Martin said.

Jerzy flashed his torch around.

'Must have been nice in its day but it's a right tip now.'

Jerzy was right, debris filled half of the corridor and some of the floor boards were missing. Martin opened the nearest door and looked inside. The builders had made a start alright as all of the floorboards were missing.

'Jerzy best not go any farther, it's obviously not safe up here. Have you got any tape you can put across the stairs on the floor below to warn the students not to go any further?'

'Yeah sure, I've got something in one of my cases that will do the job nicely.'

Martin was quite glad to make it back down to where it was well lit. He waited while Jerzy went and got the tape. He returned a few minutes later holding a large roll of blue and white striped tape. He wrapped it around the bannister on the left and then pulled it so it was taut and then did the same to the bannister on the right. Martin was only able to read what on it when Jerzy stepped back.

Police Line Do Not Cross, it said in bold blue letters.

'Bloody hell, Jerzy! Where did you get that from?' Martin exclaimed.

'Well you know, people leave things lying around,' Jerzy answered with a shrug of the shoulders.

Martin decided not to pursue the subject further. Anyway he had to admit that Jerzy was right, it did do the job nicely.

'Okay then let's have a look at the cellar,' Martin said.

They went downstairs and opened the door to the beer cellar. There was a light switch and Martin tried it. He wasn't surprised when it didn't work. He'd only gone down five or six steps when Jerzy shouted at him to stop.

'Look boss!' he said shining his torch towards the end of the stairs.

Three of the lower steps were missing, not only that but the wooden stairs had begun to sway slightly as they moved. Martin and Jerzy beat a hasty retreat.

'More tape on this door too please, Jerzy,' Martin said. 'So we've just got the bar area on the ground floor and the function room to cover. That makes it a bit easier I suppose.'

He looked at his watch. It was nearly four thirty.

'Fancy something to eat before the lab rats arrive?'

'There's a burger place just down the road,' Jerzy suggested with a smile.

Martin thought about what Liz had said.

'That'll do for me. Come on I'm buying.'

Chapter Three – The Lab Rats

She'd had trouble sleeping during the night, which wasn't all that unusual lately, and so she'd set her alarm clock forward by a few hours. She still somehow managed to sleep through it and awoke groggy and bleary eyed to find that it had just gone three o'clock in the afternoon. She got up and sat on the edge of the bed and tried to remember what day it was.

'Oh fuck!' she said out loud as she remembered that today was the day.

She'd been looking forward to the ghost hunt for weeks and it would be just like her to fuck it up. She realised that she didn't need to be at the pub until six thirty so she calmed herself down and got in the shower which was thankfully free. She put on a pair of black skinny jeans and a black T shirt over which she pulled a thick black sweater. She put on a pair of big black lace up boots and a black zip-up fleece topped off by a black woollen hat.

She poured herself a glass of orange juice and gulped it down. It was cheap concentrate and the acidity burned her throat but it did its job as she felt a little more awake. She looked at herself in the mirror and frowned. The black bags under her eyes matched her outfit. She decided to put some make up on but she wasn't sure that it helped that much. When she'd been young she'd always wanted to be pretty and she'd loved pink. Her mother, however, informed her more than once that she'd never be pretty and that only whores wore pink. She wondered what her mother would think of her present outfit.

Let's not go there, she said to herself.

She grabbed her backpack, luckily pre-packed the night before, and she was ready to go. She locked the door behind her and walked out into the street. She looked back at the shared house she'd rented with some 'friends' she'd made in her first year at university. Great friends they'd turned out to be. The bitch in the room next door had thought it was a good idea to put a heavy metal album on full blast at two in the morning. Even after it had finished, she'd kept herself awake by having fantasies about all of the different methods she could use to kill her. She'd been living in the house for four months now and she couldn't wait until her contract expired at the end of the academic year so she could move out. Anyway she'd have a couple of days away from the racket next door which, if she was honest, was also part of the reason why she'd volunteered in the first place.

She had to wait for the train into London as she'd just missed one and she hoped she wasn't cutting it too fine. She thought about the 'experiment', as the professor called it, as she sat on the train looking out of the window without seeing anything. She found that she liked Martin Jorgensen. He was different to her other tutors in being more like a big kid than a professor. He was obviously in love with what he did and it showed in his teaching. She found herself looking forward to his classes. She knew that some of the other girls on her course also looked forward to his classes but it had nothing to do with his teaching style. She'd found out recently that a couple of the men liked him in that way too. She would turn around and see them looking at the professor all gooey-eyed during lectures. She sincerely hoped that they'd all grow up some day.

However she had noticed his assistant. He looked like he might have been something in a heavy metal rock band, so definitely not her normal type, but there was something about him that attracted her. She found herself looking at him sometimes without really knowing why. He never seemed to look back though.

She got off at Kings Cross and got lost several times before she found the tube line that would take her to Finchley Road. She stood up on the crowded tube train for the short journey and checked the time on her phone. It had just gone five thirty. She pulled out the sheet she'd been given that told her how to reach the hotel. Thankfully it looked straightforward enough. She looked out of the window at the blackness of the tunnel and found that she was getting excited about what might be happening in just a couple of hours or so.

She found the hotel easily enough. It was basic but warm and clean. The thing she found hard to adjust to though was its quietness. Compared to her house she felt like she'd just had her ears stuffed with cotton wool.

She looked at the double bed. It looked comfortable and she felt tempted to get undressed and then slide her body under the thick duvet and drift off to sleep surrounded by blissful silence. She stood there for a few minutes wavering before she sighed and set off for the pub.

The alarm clock woke him at two o'clock. It only rang twice before his arm snaked out and shut it off. He sat on the edge of the bed and smiled. He felt awake and full of energy. He pulled the curtains wide and let the rays from the low winter sun enter the room. Over the past ten days or so he'd been going to bed later and later so that he'd have no problems staying awake all night for the professor's experiment.

He had little problem with sleeping as his extensive flat was in a select part of town well away from the noise of the student area. His father had insisted that he lived somewhere 'reasonable' and he had to admit that he'd been right. He visited the student area for a drink occasionally but he found it far too garish and loud. There was no way he could have lived anywhere near it.

He thought about what the night might hold as he showered. He had an idea that there might be more to it than a simple ghost hunt but that only made it all the more intriguing. The fact that it would count towards the mandatory experimental work he was supposed to carry out made it even better as it looked like it might actually be amusing.

He had his usual breakfast of black coffee, wholemeal toast and muesli and kept his eye on the clock. He put his freshly ironed blue jeans on, a new white T shirt and then pulled a thick woollen Arran jumper over that. A pair of spotless white trainers, a grey waxed jacket topped off with a grey beanie hat with a designer logo prominently displayed on the front and he was ready. He picked up his backpack and looked at it. It was quite full but he still wondered if he had everything he needed. He went to the fridge and got a large bottle of water that he put in a pocket on the outside. Now he was ready. He left right on time and reached the station exactly five minutes before his train was due.

He looked at the timetable he'd created. He should be at the hotel no later than ten past five and that would give plenty of time to empty his backpack and stow everything away before he had to be at the pub.

The train was bang on time. He smiled as it rattled towards London. He was on schedule and everything was in control, just as he liked it.

The radio alarm woke her and she lay back with her eyes closed trying to puzzle it out. It wasn't her usual morning programme. Where the bloody hell had Grimmy gone? Then she remembered.

Oh, the bloody experiment's tonight, she grumpily reminded herself.

She opened an eye and looked at the clock, it was two thirty. She made herself sit up but it took an effort. When she did it felt like her brain was banging from one side of her skull to the other. She felt dreadful and tried to remember what had happened the night before.

It all suddenly came back and her face flushed red with embarrassment. She had decided that, as she didn't have to get up early, she'd make a night of it with some friends. Then she'd met this beautiful young man in a nightclub and she was all set for a night of wonderful sex when the three double Baileys that she'd just knocked back returned with even more force that they'd gone down. She threw up all over his designer shirt. He didn't look impressed and that was the last she'd seen of him. She couldn't remember how she'd gotten home.

She dragged herself into the shower hoping it would wake her up a bit. She did feel a little better afterwards. She went to the fridge and drank near enough a whole carton of orange juice and, while it made her feel a little less dehydrated, it didn't sit well in her stomach.

She wondered what to wear. The professor had warned that it might be cold but she decided to ignore his warning. She put some tights on and then pulled on a short purple patterned skirt. She pulled on a low cut vest and a jumper that was low enough to show off her cleavage and tight enough so the boys could see what she had to offer. She put on a fur collared coat that was also low cut. She smiled at herself in the mirror and blew herself a kiss.

She rummaged around the untidy room until she found her backpack which had been hiding underneath the bed. She grabbed a handful of items from each of her drawers and scrunched them inside. Her makeup bag, a box of paracetamol, a half-bottle of vodka, some knickers and a couple of condoms, just in case, and she was ready to go.

It was sunny outside which was fine as it meant that she could hide her bleary eyes behind a pair of sunglasses. She got to the station two minutes late but thankfully so did the train. As the train rattled on its way into London she thought about the 'experiment' for probably only the third time. The first was when she'd seen the poster on the Psychology Faculty notice board. It would count towards her course and it looked like fun but best of all was when she found out that she and the scrumptious professor might be staying in the same hotel together. She'd decided at the start of the term that she was going to get him into bed if it killed her.

The second time she thought about it was when she got invited to the interview. Even though it was only open to second year students they'd had loads of applicants and so she was surprised when she got the letter confirming her place. She could only put it down to the fact that the dreamy Martin must fancy her. After all her marks hadn't exactly been stunning in her first year and her tutor had reminded her several times that being in university should be more about studying than having a good time.

She was finding it hard though. She knew she was intelligent enough, she wouldn't be in university otherwise, but she found turning down a night out to be just about impossible at times. A night out for her and her friends usually meant having far too much to drink culminating in a night of sex. It hadn't quite worked out the night before so now she was in the position of not having had sex for a whole week.

She thought of his cute bum and smiled. Perhaps it might be just as well, saving it all up for a night of lust with the professor might be well worth waiting for.

He woke up feeling a bit groggy and had a problem remembering what he'd done the night before. He almost laughed when he did. Of course he'd been doing some research on the psychology of memory and especially on how it was retrieved. He'd done his homework and in the last week or so he'd read everything the professor had published. He had an inkling that the real 'experiment' might be a little different to that advertised. While the students might be looking for ghosts he had an idea that the professor might be watching them instead.

He'd never been the subject of an experiment before and the whole idea appealed to him greatly. Indeed he thought that this might potentially be as important as the Stanford or Stanley Milgram experiments and being part of something historic like that would be truly mind-blowing.

He'd woken early enough to cram in a few hours reading before he had to go. He wanted to read up on a few articles he'd come across on group dynamics. Even though there would only be six of them he'd decided that he'd conduct his own little experiment on how all the members of the group interacted with each other. He was certain that the professor would be doing this too.

He made himself a pot of strong coffee and got stuck in. As always he became so engrossed that time just flew by. He was glad that he'd set the alarm clock again. He had just enough time to shower, pack and dress. He made sure his backpack had more than enough notepads and pens. He put his precious tablet in there too as he reckoned he'd have quite a bit of downtime and he'd downloaded lots of academic papers that he thought might be relevant.

He then pulled on the same pair of black jeans he'd wore the day before and probably the day before that too, then an old Thin Lizzie T shirt over which he pulled a thick dark blue fleece. He put on an old pair of scuffed steel toe capped boots, bought not for protection but because they were cheap and would last. He then put on his old green fish-tail parka, which he lived in during winter, and topped it off with a baseball cap. He'd found the cap in a charity shop the week before and he just couldn't resist it. It featured a distressed looking ghost looking out of a red roundel with a thick red diagonal stripe across it.

He smiled at it as he looked in the mirror. He hoped that the professor would get the joke too.

He hadn't bothered looking up the times of the trains, they went often enough and he'd allowed lots of time to get there. As he sat on the train and watched the buildings go by he thought about the professor. At first he'd dismissed him as being somewhat shallow and popularist. After all his lectures were always full, mostly because they were amusing and quite simple, simple on the surface that is. As he read more of the professor's work he became aware that, if you looked at what he was saying in a slightly different way, it was really quite deep and even unsettling at times.

The 'experiment' was a case in point. He thought it might actually be an experiment disguised as an experiment disguised as yet another experiment. Of course one experiment was as advertised, a simple two night ghost hunt in a haunted pub that was going to use the latest technology to see if any evidence for paranormal activity could be found and recorded. The second experiment would undoubtedly be observing the group to see how they reacted in a stressful situation, what beliefs and goals became shared and what social cohesion occurred or didn't occur. He was certain that he would be identified as the 'black sheep' but he was used to that.

It was the third experiment that had him really hooked though. At the end of his last paper the professor had hinted that there might be a new approach to examining many so-called 'paranormal' events, an approach that could be tested by experiment.

He was hoping that this would be the experiment that the professor had hinted at.

He just couldn't wait to see what it was all about.

Chapter Four – They all meet

Martin had always marvelled at what Jerzy managed to fit into his cases. They'd come back after stuffing down a double burger and fries each when, without a word, Jerzy produced an electric kettle, a large container of water, a four pint bottle of milk, a massive catering pack of teabags and a sleeve full of plastic cups. He then fiddled around inside the case before triumphantly producing a teaspoon.

Martin didn't ask where all this had come from but he suspected that the university catering department might be a little light on their next inventory.

'You're a mind reader Jerzy,' Martin said as he watched his assistant set up the kettle. 'I'm glad you remembered to bring all this along.'

'No problem. We've got pretty much everything we need, milk, tea, some drinking chocolate and instant coffee to help keep us all awake but there's a problem with the biscuits.'

'Biscuits?'

'Yes I could only get custard creams,' Jerzy replied as he pulled out the biggest box of biscuits Martin had ever seen.

Martin laughed out loud.

'God, whatever we're paying you is nowhere near enough.'

'Too bloody true,' Jerzy said, 'so any chance of a pay rise?'

'If I could get you more I would believe me but if we're successful and get a paper out of this, then you never know. It might just give us a bit of leverage with the powers that be.'

Jerzy handed Martin a plastic cup of tea and then offered his as a toast.

'To success,' Jerzy said.

'To success,' Martin echoed.

'So how much are you going to tell them?'

Martin gave it some thought.

'I'm only going to tell them that this is a ghost hunt. I mean I'm still interested to see if we get anything out of the ordinary especially after speaking to Pat Whelan. I'm sure that some of them will figure out that we'll be observing them as a group, after all they are psychology students, but I don't want any of them knowing the real reason we're here. It might skew the results if they do.'

'Well they might twig when you start asking them questions.'

'Yes that might give the game away so I've decided to get them to write it all down rather than do that and it'll be quicker too. Anyway there'll be a lot going on and I'm hoping that a bit of cognitive overload might occur to stop them thinking too deeply.'

They were interrupted by someone knocking at the door. Jerzy went over and opened it and ushered in a young man. He was slim and of medium height with a beard that needed trimming and long hair sticking out of the sides of a black baseball cap. The cap had the 'Ghostbusters' logo on the front.

'Very good that,' Martin said with a smile as he pointed towards the cap. 'Jerzy this is Josh Tyler originally from Birmingham. Josh this is my assistant Jerzy Kowalski.'

The two men shook hands.

'Cup of tea, Josh?' Jerzy asked.

'Oh yes please!' Josh replied with a grin. 'It's bloody freezing out there.'

'Have you checked in yet?' Martin asked.

'Oh yes, the hotel's not bad is it? A lot better than my place anyway.'

Josh sat down at the table next to Martin. He pulled out a notepad and pen.

'Taking notes then,' Martin said.

'Well yes, I always like to have a notepad handy.'

'You'll be taking notes on us all I take it. I know that group dynamics is one of your interests.'

Josh hesitated. He was surprised that the professor had guessed what he was up to so quickly and didn't know whether to deny it or not. He decided not to.

'Well yes, I thought it would be a good opportunity to see how it worked in real life. That's okay isn't it?' he said hoping that he'd made the right choice.

'That's better than okay. If you're serious about being a psychologist you should never miss an opportunity to observe. I'll tell you what, if you're willing to share and you come up with something interesting, I'll incorporate it into the final report and give you credit. What do you think?'

'Brilliant! That's great, thanks Professor Jorgensen,' Josh said with a smile than ran from ear to ear.

'It's Martin while we're here Josh and let's keep this arrangement strictly between the three of us, okay?'

They were interrupted by another knock on the door. Jerzy opened the door again and let in a girl dressed all in black. She was no more than five feet five tall and at first glance might have been taken for being younger than she actually was.

'Lydia, welcome to the Black Vaults. As you can see it's just the place to be on a Saturday night.'

'Hi Professor Jorgensen,' she said in a light Scottish accent as she unzipped her fleece. She looked around the room. 'Oh well I've been in worse pubs than this.'

This made Martin smile.

'Cup of tea?' Jerzy asked.

'Yes please,' she replied.

'So Lydia this is my assistant Jerzy Kowalski, Jerzy this is Lydia McGillivray from Edinburgh.'

Jerzy and Lydia nodded and smiled at each other. Jerzy thought she looked different when she smiled. She looked far too serious when she wasn't.

'Where are you from?' Lydia asked.

'Who me?' Jerzy asked surprised at the question.

Lydia nodded.

'From Ealing,' he replied.

'Oh, I'm sorry. I just thought that with your name...' she said lamely.

'Oh that! Well my parents come from a little town not far from Warsaw but I was born after they came here.'

'Oh,' she said, looking somewhat uncomfortable.

'By the way do you know Josh?' Martin asked, helping her out.

'Not really but I've seen him around the campus though, mostly in the library. Hi Josh,' she said.

'Hi Lydia,' Josh replied as he made a note in his notepad.

Martin looked at his watch. It was six twenty. Ten minutes later there was another knock on the door. Martin opened it this time as Jerzy and Josh were talking.

'Hello Jonathan! You made it and right on time as usual,' Martin said.

'Well it did say six thirty in the plan.'

A tall sandy haired young man came in and looked around the room. He wore glasses with thick black rims and his face had a permanent expression of slight puzzlement stamped on it.

'Cup of tea?' Jerzy asked.

'Oh no thank you, I never drink tea. Do you have any coffee?'

'Yes but it's only instant I'm afraid.'

'That's okay then, I'll just have some water.'

Jerzy made to pour some from the large container into a cup when Jonathan stopped him.

'It's okay I've brought my own,' he said pulling the water bottle from his backpack.

'Well, let me introduce you,' Martin said as he ushered Jonathan towards the rest of the team.

'This is my assistant Jerzy and this is Lydia and this is Josh.'

'Hi Jonathan, how's it going?' Josh asked. 'We've got the same tutor,' he explained to the team.

Jonathan just nodded towards Josh. They obviously weren't exactly best friends.

Martin continued, 'Well for the rest of you this is Jonathan Conyngham who's from London if I remember right.'

Jonathan corrected Martin.

'Well, Kensington actually.'

Martin almost felt sorry for him. From what he'd seen of Jonathan he was sure that there was no harm in him, however, looking at the reactions of the rest of the team he could see that their first impressions of him might not have been all that positive.

They chatted with periods of awkward silence that Martin did his best to fill. They had to wait another fifteen minutes before the last member of the team arrived. Martin opened the door and a very blonde girl with a very short skirt and fur collared jacket gyrated in.

'Everyone this is Madison Symons who's from St. Albans,' Martin said.

He watched the reaction of the other members. Jerzy, Jonathan and Josh all looked quite interested to say the least. After all even

Martin had to admit that Madison was quite pretty and she had a really nice body. She knew it too and he couldn't help noticing the way that she swayed her hips as she moved towards the table. Her wide smile was only aimed at the males present, Lydia was totally ignored.

Martin had wondered about including Madison. He knew that she'd be a disruptive influence and would probably end up in bed with one of the men in the group before long. But again, like Jonathan, he thought there might be more to her than the shallow exterior that she put on like a costume. On seeing her again he had some doubts about his decision but there was nothing he could do about it now.

'Okay first off we all go by first names here including me. So everyone this is Madison, Madison this is my assistant Jerzy.'

Madison looked Jerzy up and down. He could see from her expression that she wasn't impressed.

'And this is Lydia.'

Madison gave her a peremptory glance only.

'This is Josh.'

Same expression as for Jerzy.

'And this is Jonathan.'

Madison didn't even look in his direction. She sat down and gave Martin a flashing smile and a look that said that she was more than a little interested.

Good God, Martin thought, Liz was right, I might have to lock my door after all.

'Okay now that everyone's here let's go over what we're going to be doing tonight. That's 'Night One' in the plan you were given.'

A rustling of papers ensued as plans were pulled out of bags. Madison didn't bother she just moved closer to Josh and looked at his.

Here we go, Martin thought, as he clocked Josh's embarrassed expression. Josh's gaze kept wandering from the plan to Madison's cleavage and Martin found his own gaze lingering there a little too long as well.

'Okay so first some explanations about this place. First the history, the pub was built in the 1850s at a time when travel from London was getting easier and people had started commuting. The area really took off in the early 1860s when the railway arrived and this pub became something of a social hub for the area. You'd probably best describe its clientele at the time as upper working and lower middle class. The pub did quite well until the fifties when it started to go downhill and it was finally shut in the eighties. It's stayed shut ever since.'

'Why was that?' Josh asked.

'No-one seems to know. The family who owned it during that time refused to sell which was surprising as it's a prime bit of real estate.'

'Do you think that it had anything to do with the reason we're here?' Lydia asked.

Martin looked at Lydia with some respect.

'As I say no-one's sure but in the will the former owners advised that the pub should be demolished so I'll let you make your own mind up about that.'

'So what's the exact reason we're here?' Lydia persisted.

'I was coming to that. The people who inherited the pub sold it to a well-known pub chain. They were going to renovate the pub and call it 'The Frog and All'.'

This elicited a small groan from the team.

'Yes I think that the new name probably needs some work too. Anyway they had a crew of builders in here who were working around the clock stripping the place down ready for the renovations. However that only lasted for a week or so after which they all walked out. They told their employers that the place was haunted and, in their words, they were 'scared shitless' and refused to go back even when they got offered a lot more money. I met one of them earlier today. He's six feet six and he definitely doesn't look like the type of man who would scare easily. However he wouldn't even set foot in the place to show me where the power switches were. So, in something of a panic, the pub chain got a priest in to do an exorcism but I'm afraid that didn't work out too well either.'

'What happened?' Jonathan asked, his face showing some concern.

'Let's just say that he ended up being scared shitless too. Now it would appear that something genuine might be going on here and so if any of you want to withdraw then I'll understand.'

The team all looked at each other but no-one made a move.

'Okay but just remember if it all gets too much for you the door's there and you can leave at any time.'

'So what exactly did they say was happening here?' Lydia asked.

Martin shrugged.

'I don't know. No-one would talk about it so, if I'm being honest, I'm not really sure what we're up against.'

'Exciting isn't it?' Jerzy said with a big smile.

The rest of the team smiled too.

Thank you Jerzy, Martin said to himself.

'If there is any paranormal activity going on do we have any idea what might have caused it?' Josh asked. 'I know that it's often reported to occur in places where traumatic events have taken place.'

'Yes that's possibly at least partly true. I've done some research and we suspect that something along those lines might have occurred here but I'll tell you all about that at the end of the experiment. I don't want to plant any ideas in your minds that might skew the results. Okay now for some Health and Safety. This place looks safe enough, as the builders didn't get too far along with their work, but please confine your activities to this floor and the function room above. We've taped off the cellar and the second floor as these are unsafe and under no circumstances are you to go near them. Is that understood?'

The team all nodded in unison including Jerzy which he found interesting.

'The centre of the unusual activity appears to be in the function room upstairs. So the bar area here is where you'll be staying while you wait to go up for your session and it's where you'll write up your notes after you've finished. It's not exactly warm but we'll keep a heater on at all times so it shouldn't get too bad. We've got a heater on upstairs but I'm afraid that it and all electrically powered items will have to be switched off during the sessions so it might get a little chilly which is why I suggested that you might want to dress in some warm clothes,' Martin said looking at Madison. 'However that doesn't include our recording equipment of course but that's been specially constructed by Jerzy to be as low powered as possible.'

'Why is that such a problem?' Lydia asked.

Martin was beginning to warm to Lydia. She was asking some good questions.

'Jerzy, do you want to answer that one?' Martin said.

'Well, have you ever wondered why ghosts are only usually seen at night or in low light conditions?' Jerzy said.

They looked at each other but no-one answered.

'One theory is that it's something to do with energy,' Jerzy continued. 'You can't see stars during the daytime because the light energy of the sun is far, far greater and it basically swamps the feeble rays that we get from distant stars. We think that it might be the same for unusual phenomena. It might be that they mainly occur at night because their energy levels are so low that any sort of light or electrical energy would swamp them. So in order to observe them we need to keep the observation space dark and as free from electrical energy as possible.'

'That's interesting, I never thought of that,' Jonathan commented.

Martin noticed that Madison's knees were already knocking together with the cold. She hadn't exactly dressed sensibly. Martin nodded to Jerzy who went to one of the cases and pulled out a blanket. He gave it to Madison who immediately wrapped it around her legs.

'Thanks,' she said with a grateful smile. 'Have you got a bed in there too?'

'No, you're lucky I've got that. I use the blankets to keep the equipment from being damaged when it's in transit,' Jerzy replied.

'Okay I now need you all to give Jerzy your mobile phones,' Martin said. 'He'll make sure that they're switched off and kept in a safe place, one that you won't be able to access so there'll be no point in looking for them. You'll get them back in the morning but I'm afraid that you'll have to go cold turkey for the next ten hours or so.'

While Jonathan, Josh and Lydia handed over their phones quite readily Madison hung onto hers. In the end Jerzy more or less had to pull it out of her hand. She gave him a sullen look as he did so.

'So the first task for you all tonight is to observe and help Jerzy set up the equipment upstairs. Please do exactly as Jerzy says as some of the kit is very delicate. He'll explain what each piece is and what it does as he goes along. It will take at least a couple of hours to set up and test everything so we should be ready for our first session sometime after ten o'clock. If you look at your plan you'll see that tonight we're doing it in pairs. There will be four sessions in all each of which will be forty five minutes long.'

'I thought they'd be a bit longer than that,' Josh commented.

'Believe me three quarters of an hour sitting silently in a dark room will feel more three hours and it is bloody cold up there as well. So we're going to start with Lydia and Madison and then it will be Josh and Jonathan's turn. That should take us up to around one thirty. After that we'll have an hour off to grab something to eat and decompress a bit. We'll turn the heater on upstairs while we're doing this. Then it will be Madison and Josh and finally Lydia and Jonathan. Jerzy and I will also be upstairs for all of the sessions.'

'So what do we actually have to do while we're up there?' Madison asked with a puzzled expression.

'Nothing except observe. There'll be no talking unless it's absolutely necessary. Jerzy will issue each of you with a notepad and a red light torch. The torches you'll be using will be quite small but should give enough light so you can see what you're writing while Jerzy and I will have some bigger versions. Being red the torch shouldn't interfere with your night vision.'

'Isn't that the same type of torch that astronomers use?' Lydia asked.

'Exactly. It will take you a few minutes for your eyes to adjust but once they do I want you to write down anything to see, hear, smell or sense in any way. We want everything, changes in emotions, any thoughts you have, even if it's just to say that you're bored. Don't edit your thoughts and feelings, just get it straight down on paper. Is that clear?'

Martin could see a thoughtful smile cross Josh's face as he said this. Martin wondered if he was getting an idea about what they were really here for.

'As soon as you finish each session I'll collect all the notes you've made and I then want you to go down here and construct another set of notes detailing again everything you've experienced during the session.'

'Is that going to be some sort of memory experiment?' Jonathan asked.

'Yes you're not far off there,' Martin said without giving any further explanation. 'So once you've written up your notes you can relax and have a drink down here until your next session. Is that okay?'

'What about loos?' Madison asked.

'Oh yes, they're a bit primitive I'm afraid. The ladies and gents on this floor are sort of usable but I'd save up anything, er...'

'Number twos?' Jerzy suggested.

'Yes exactly. Well I'd save those up for the hotel if you possibly can. Okay so over to you Jerzy.'

Martin looked on as the team gathered around Jerzy and one of the cases.

So far so good, he thought. Josh might have a clue, but he more or less expected that, as for the rest he was fairly sure that they still thought that they were just on a ghost hunt.

Chapter Five – The Cold Spot

The group gathered around Jerzy as he began unpacking the cases.

'So what have you got?' Josh asked his eyes widening as handheld devices, cameras and phones were unpacked and placed on the table.

'Well the prof and I decided early on to keep it fairly simple. I know there are some teams who try to cover absolutely everything possible but then again they've probably got the money to do it,' Jerzy said a shrug.

'Unfortunately the university isn't that generous when it comes to equipment,' Martin said, 'so Jerzy's had to improvise. However I honestly think that what he's come up with is one of the best recording systems for this of type of work that I've ever seen.'

Jerzy's face went a little red at Martin's praise but he meant every word of it.

'What's so special about it?' Lydia asked.

'Well we looked at all the evidence before we started doing this and we decided to concentrate on three things, vision, sound and temperature,' Jerzy replied. 'So the stuff we've bought includes thermal imaging and low light cameras and some really nice microphones.'

'So what about EMF?' Josh asked.

'We don't bother with that stuff,' Jerzy said dismissively. 'That's what the ghost hunters on

TV use but it's all rubbish. There's never been a proven link between electromagnetic fields and unusual phenomena so even if you picked up something it wouldn't mean anything.'

'What are all the phones for?' Jonathan said with a puzzled look.

'That's the really ingenious bit,' Martin replied. 'Jerzy put up a poster asking students to donate their old smart phones when they upgraded. He's coded an app which has basically turned them into motion and sound sensors so, if anything moves the phone camera goes off, but the really great thing is, as we have so many, we can cover a really large area. They also react to sound too which is really useful.'

'But wouldn't the microphones be more sensitive?' Jonathan asked.

'Of course they'll capture any sound but the phones can help with confirming the exact directionality,' Jerzy explained. 'I feed their exact location into the computer and then the programme can tell us what's going on. There'll be a tiny lag between the times that each phone reacts so we can tell where the sound is coming from and, if it's moving, then we can accurately track it.'

'The main reason why I said it was good though is that, through some really clever programming, Jerzy's been able to link everything we've got into a single system. He's built a dashboard that displays all the vision and sound streams as well as the temperature data on the same screen. Everything is downloaded onto a computer in real time so one person can keep an eye on everything that's happening. We also obviously record all the data so we can do some detailed research after the event. You'll get to have a little play with it later,' Martin said.

Jerzy shot Martin a look.

'Under Jerzy's supervision of course and please follow his orders to the letter and be careful. Our equipment fund is next to nothing until next term so try not to break anything. Okay Jerzy, where do you want to start?'

The team all turned and looked at Jerzy.

'It's quite a big space up there so we need to see if we can identify any particular areas that we might need to concentrate on. So what we'll do first is use a thermal imaging camera to sweep the room and see if we can identify anything unusual.'

'You're looking for cold spots,' Josh said.

'Yes, that's right. I've also got this neat bit of gear, it's a hand held mic that's really sensitive and its range is really good so it will pick up very low frequency sounds as well as high. We can do a sweep with that too. If we don't spot anything we'll have to try and cover the whole room which will be a bit more of a challenge.'

Jerzy picked up two hand held devices, turned them on and then set them up.

'Okay, so this is the thermal imaging camera.'

They gathered tightly around Jerzy and looked at the small screen. Martin couldn't help noticing that they were now hanging on his every word.

'Okay so here you can see the prof, here's the heater. If we go from one to the other you can see that the colour is much more intense for the heater. The display at the bottom of the screen shows the temperature but, once you've used this for a bit, you can tell what it is just from the colour alone. Now if we look out into the bar area you can see that all the colours have changed. The coldest spot is that far corner at around six degrees or so and that's just about what we'd expect. Pass it around but be careful.'

Jerzy gave it to Josh first who seemed somewhat reluctant to pass it on to Jonathan. Lydia then had a look and finally Madison who only glanced at it. Martin could tell that she was getting a little bored already.

'Now this is the mic. If it picks up anything you'll hear it through the headphones. Of course it will pick up sounds that are beyond our hearing range but what's really clever about it is that it translates whatever it picks up into a sound we can hear. So just be aware that what you're hearing might not be exactly what the mic is picking up. A word of caution, when this is in operation everyone please keep as quiet as possible.'

'What if it picks up a really loud noise? Would we be deafened if we have the headphones on?' Jonathan asked.

'No, it would still sound loud of course but the system automatically reduces the volume so it's quite safe,' Jerzy replied.

'Okay shall we go and see what's up there?' Martin said.

The team trooped up the stairs after Jerzy in single file. Martin followed behind and he once again thought how blessed he'd been when Jerzy had turned up in his class a few years before. As he climbed up the stairs he was aware of a mounting tension and excitement inside him. After a series of fairly disappointing investigations was this finally going to be the one?

They all entered the function room very quietly and looked around. Even though the heater had been on for a while it still felt cold.

'Bit of a dump isn't it?' Madison said with a pout.

'Yes but the great thing is that for the next couple of nights it's our dump,' Martin replied with a smile.

'It doesn't feel that spooky to me,' Madison continued with another disappointed look.

Josh had somehow ended up with the thermal imaging camera again and he started doing a sweep of the room.

'Who wants to try the mic?' Jerzy asked.

Lydia put her hand up. At that moment Martin thought that she looked like the clever kid in class who always knew the answer to every question.

'Okay just hold this and then put the headphones on,' Jerzy said. Then in a louder voice, 'Everyone quiet!'

He turned the mic on and Lydia started sweeping the room. Martin could see that Josh was getting a bit agitated about something but he signed for him to wait until Lydia had finished.

'Hear anything?' Jerzy whispered.

'Yes loads of things,' Lydia said quite loudly.

Her own voice made her jump so she continued in a near whisper.

'It sounds quiet in here but it's really noisy with the headphones on. I'm sure I heard a bus go by somewhere.'

'Yes it's really sensitive. I think you might need to use it for a while before you can really sort out what it is you're actually hearing.'

'Er... Jerzy?' Josh interrupted giving him a worried look. 'I think this might be broken or something.'

Jerzy scowled and then signed for Lydia to take the headphones off. He went over and snatched the camera from Josh. He looked at the screen and then moved the camera from side to side. He then walked towards the far end of the room and stopped.

'Christ prof, I think you need to see this!' Jerzy said.

Martin knew from his assistant's tone of voice that he'd found something. He scurried over and Jerzy showed him what was on the camera screen. He saw an intensely dark column that ran from the floor to the ceiling. Jerzy reset the range on the camera to increase the resolution. They walked around in a circle and looked at the column from several directions.

'What is it?' Josh asked.

Martin didn't answer. He tentatively put his hand into the column and withdrew it quickly. He breathed out and his breath turned icy white.

'It's a cold spot. It looks like it's round and approximately four feet across. It seems to run from the floor right up to the ceiling like a column. What temperature is it Jerzy?' Martin asked as he handed the camera back.

'The temperature gradient in the room is all over the place. It's warmer nearer the heater and cold in the far corners but that column, it's minus eleven, that's nearly fifteen degrees colder than the coldest spot in the room.'

'Is that unusual?' Lydia asked.

'Well, I've never seen anything like this before,' Jerzy replied. 'How about you, prof?'

Martin shook his head.

'No this is really strange. The thing about heat is that, in a gas such as air, it should cause convection and the warmer and colder air should mix. Even if there was some sort of a forced draught and cold air was being blown in the room it should still be blurry at the edges as it mixes with the warmer air.'

Martin stood looking thoughtfully at the cold spot. He put his hand in again and withdrew it again quickly. It was really cold.

'And that's not like that?' Jonathan asked.

Martin shook his head.

'No the edges are clean and well defined and the column seems to be totally static. Believe me this is really strange. Well Jerzy I think we've discovered where you need to set up your equipment. If you cover this end of the room then we can set up some chairs and a table at the other end and observe from there. I take it that your cabling will reach okay?'

'Oh God yes, I've got about two hundred feet of cable downstairs.'

Last time they'd done this Jerzy had been moaning that he only had fifty feet of cable and it wasn't enough. Martin didn't want to know where he'd got the other hundred and fifty feet from.

'Cabling is a bit old fashioned, isn't it? Couldn't you just use wireless?' Josh asked.

'Well we could but it's this energy thing again, isn't it?' Jerzy replied. 'Okay wifi's energy intensity is really low but we can't be sure whether it would affect the phenomena we want to observe or not. Anyway we think it's not worth taking the chance.'

Josh nodded and smiled.

'Okay let's go back down and get everything upstairs,' Jerzy said. 'But carefully mind, very carefully.'

It took them just over two hours to get everything positioned and linked up. There were two sensitive microphones, positioned on low stands about four feet from the walls on either side of the cold spot. Two cameras, one thermal imaging and one low light, were moving in an arc slowly from side to side each one covering the whole of the lower part of the room. Then twenty phones on little stands were dotted around the cold spot so that every angle was covered. Wires from all the recorders were bundled together and they ran down to the other end of the room into a jury-rigged black box that was then connected to Jerzy's laptop.

'Well done everyone,' Martin said. 'There's nothing broken so you've made my assistant a very happy man.'

Jerzy didn't respond. His eyes were glued to his computer screen as his fingers flashed across the keyboard.

'Okay it will take Jerzy a little while to check that everything's working properly so we might as well go back downstairs and get ourselves a hot drink,' Martin suggested.

Madison led the way. She was shivering with the cold and he could see that she was anxious to get back to where it was a little warmer. She made straight for the heater as soon as she got downstairs.

'I'll just be a minute,' Martin said before he disappeared out of the front door.

He walked quickly back to where his car was parked and got an old donkey jacket that he kept in the boot in case he had to work on the car when it was cold or if he ever had a breakdown. He shook it and then made his way back to the pub. He locked the door behind him and then gave the coat to Madison.

'It's not very fashionable I'm afraid but it will keep you a bit warmer. Make sure you bring the blanket up with you for your legs when you go upstairs. Dying from fright is within the parameters of the experiment but dying from pneumonia definitely isn't.'

Madison took the coat from him and gratefully put it on. She buttoned it up and then pulled the collar to her nose and smelt it. When she looked up at Martin her eyes had an explicit invitation in them. Again he began to wonder if him staying in the same hotel as her had been a wise thing to do.

Lydia started making drinks for everyone. She gave Josh a steaming cup of coffee and then Jonathan who accepted it gratefully. He'd obviously decided that instant might be drinkable after all. She placed a cup near Madison who was still defrosting herself at the heater before handing Martin one.

'Thanks Lydia. Look I'm not expecting you to have to make the drinks you know...'

'Worried about stereotypes? The wee woman being made to feel subservient and all that?' she asked with a smile. 'No I honestly don't mind, I like to keep busy. I must admit to being a bit nervous though. What do you think will happen when we go up there?'

'I've no idea and to tell you the truth I'm a little bit nervous too,' Martin admitted.

'How many of these experiments have you carried out?' Lydia asked.

Martin could see that Josh and Jonathan were listening closely to their conversation.

'Oh over twenty or so I should think, over about six or seven years that is.'

'And in all of those you've never seen a cold spot like that before?'

Martin shook his head.

'Not even close.'

He looked at the team and they could see some concern on his face.

'Look, it's okay for Jerzy and me, we know what we're getting ourselves into or at least we think we do. As I've said before if anything happens up there and you get freaked out by it you're free to go at any time.'

They all looked at each other.

'Well I came here in the hope that something actually would happen,' Josh said with certainty, 'so if it does I'm not going anywhere.'

Jonathan and Lydia didn't say anything.

'What are you talking about?' Madison said as she rejoined the group.

'I'm just reminding everyone that if it gets a bit too scary up there then you're free to go at any time,' Martin said.

'Scary? Like what?' Madison said with a puzzled expression.

'No idea.'

'God I thought it would be like the ghost hunts you see on the telly with us all running around, swearing and getting excited. All we'll really be doing is sitting in silence in an old dump of a pub room. The only thing I'm scared of is being bored stiff,' Madison said with a disappointed face.

'I've got a feeling that this is going to be anything but boring,' Martin said.

'Well, whatever, I'll be glad when it's over. I can't wait until we get back to the hotel.'

The look she gave him coupled with the slight emphasis on the word 'we' made it clear that she expected some excitement when they got back to the hotel. Martin sighed and started chanting the name of Barry Walker in his head to remind himself of the consequences that might ensue.

Lydia had obviously picked up what was going on and couldn't help giving him a questioning glance. He gave her a resigned shrug of the shoulders as a response. He'd had an idea that Madison might end up in bed with someone but the thought that he might be her target had never entered his mind. He remembered his wife's warning and decided to do exactly what she'd recommended and lock his door.

He was relieved when Jerzy shouted from the top of the stairs that he was ready. At that moment he would have sooner faced a horde of ghosts than have to put up with any more of Madison's amorous looks.

'Don't forget your torches and notebooks,' Martin said to Lydia and Madison. 'Oh and of course your blanket, Madison.'

'Oh call me Mad, everyone I know calls me Mad.'

Martin could well believe it.

Chapter Six – Session 1: Lydia and Madison

Jerzy was once again glued to his laptop screen and never even glanced in Martin's direction when he asked if everything was ready.

'I just need to tweak something,' Jerzy replied. Then a few seconds later, 'Okay I think we're ready to go.'

Martin turned to the two girls who were sitting next to each other at a table a few feet away to the right of Jerzy.

'Madison, Lydia, are you okay?' When they both nodded Martin continued. 'Right make sure your pens and notebooks are at the ready and your torches are turned on.'

Martin turned his own torch on too and then went over and turned all the lights off. He used the torch to navigate back to the seat next to Jerzy who handed him a set of headphones. He turned the torch off and, apart from computer display and the thin red beams of the girls' torches, they were plunged into darkness.

'You may hear me and Jerzy whispering from time to time but please don't talk unless you have too,' Martin said. 'Remember if things get too scary just shout and I'll immediately put the lights back on.'

Martin and Jerzy kept their eyes on the computer screen. The thermal imaging camera clearly showed the cold spot as it scanned the room. It looked real on the screen, as if it were a stone column holding the roof up. The low light camera showed nothing at all. They'd been sitting there for exactly six minutes when they picked up a distinct noise.

Martin thought that it sounded like breathing, an animal of some sort perhaps? He became excited, were the manifestations starting already?

'Did you hear that?' Jerzy wrote on a notepad.

'Yes,' Martin wrote back.

In the reflected light he could see that Jerzy had taken off his headphones and was flashing his torch towards where the girls were sitting.

'What is it?' Martin whispered.

He didn't need a reply as Jerzy's torch picked out Madison who was slumped on the table and was fast asleep. She was lightly snoring. The torch also picked out Lydia who made the action of shaking with both hands. Martin understood that she was asking him if he wanted her to wake Madison up. Martin shook his head.

'I can try and filter her out so we won't hear her in the headphones if you want,' Jerzy whispered.

Martin nodded. He put on the headphones again and Madison's snoring started to slowly fade away and then it disappeared altogether. Martin gave Jerzy the thumbs up. He looked at the clock on the computer. Eight minutes had gone.

The time went slowly by and the displays on the screen stayed unchanged. Then the sound waveform display started to show some very small peaks. Martin listened as hard as he could but he had to wait until the peaks got quite a bit larger before he could hear it. Even then it was incredibly faint and muffled. It was composed of two notes going from lower to higher.

'Hear that?' Jerzy wrote.

Martin gave him the thumbs up.

Could it be a voice? Martin thought.

He couldn't be sure but its upward inflection was like that when someone asks a question. If it was a voice it was quite high, a child's voice perhaps? Martin immediately thought of all the young girls who were probably murdered in this very room. The voice, if that was what it was, slowly faded away. Martin was left with the feeling that there was something familiar about it but he couldn't think what.

Another period of inactivity and then, at around the sixteen minute mark, Jerzy pointed to the screen. The low light camera was showing pinpoints of light near the ceiling in the vicinity of the cold spot. The thermal imaging camera showed nothing except the dark column. Jerzy adjusted the resolution and the points became brighter and then they came together to form a sort of fuzzy ball that began to move erratically around the column. Then they heard sounds.

Again it was quite faint but it was undeniably the flapping of a bird's wings.

Jerzy wrote, 'Hear a bird?'

Martin gave him the thumbs up and then listened intently. The flapping of the wings became louder as if the bird was distressed in some way. Then he heard another sound. The bird seemed to be hitting into something, glass perhaps?

'Bird trapped in here?' Martin wrote.

Jerzy scribbled a reply, 'No way, look at the TIC.'

Martin looked at the output from the thermal imaging camera but there was nothing. If a bird was trapped in the room its body heat would have shown up all too clearly on the screen.

'Working OK?' Martin wrote.

'Check after,' Jerzy replied.

The fluttering faded away and was replaced by silence.

After a couple of minutes Martin removed his headphones and he could hear Madison still snoring gently away. He put them back on just in time to catch something. He looked at the sound display and he could see some slight peaks building up.

He was listening intently when he heard a loud noise at the same time as he saw the peaks on the display shoot upwards. It was a shriek, high pitched and again as if coming from a child, but there was nothing muffled about this. Martin shone his torch in Lydia's direction. She sat as if frozen with her hand covering her mouth. She looked scared. He could see that Madison was twitching slightly but she was still fast asleep.

Martin pointed towards her asking the question with his mouth, 'You?'

She shook her head.

When he looked back Jerzy was writing something on the pad.

'Not them - came from area around cold spot.'

Martin was getting excited now. In all his other experiments he'd never come across anything remotely like this before. He looked at the clock. Only twenty seven minutes had gone.

He flashed his torch towards Lydia and mouthed 'Okay?'

She nodded and gave him a brave smile.

The seconds crawled by while the dashboard showed nothing out of the ordinary, nothing that is except the extraordinary column of icy air that stood unmoving at the far end of the room.

Martin felt the tension building in his stomach and the small hairs at the back of his neck started to stand up. The feeling reminded him of a visit to a science museum when he'd been young. He'd been fascinated by a Van der Graaff generator they had there, a metal ball that when touched made your hair stand on end. He could almost taste the static electricity in his mouth when he touched the ball. He had exactly the same metallic taste in his mouth now.

Yet nothing happened. The dashboard stayed flat and now thirty five minutes had passed by.

The tension kept building until it became almost unbearable. Martin had the same sort of skittish and uneasy feeling that he got just before a thunderstorm was about to let rip except that this was far more intense.

'Feel it?' Martin wrote, hoping it wasn't just him.

'Something's going to happen,' Jerzy replied.

Well at least it wasn't just him then.

Each second continued to crawl by, seeming to take an eternity to change on the computer's digital clock. Then they heard a sound.

Martin knew that it had started at last.

It was low and indistinct at first. He couldn't make out the words but he could hear a voice, a man's voice perhaps. It was gruff and low pitched at first and for some reason Martin felt there was a dark threat there. Then the voice became higher and louder. He could sense great anger in the voice and a sudden thrill of fear went through him that made him shudder.

Jerzy pointed to the thermal imaging screen. It showed the stolid black pillar of the cold spot but in front of it shadows that were slightly lighter in colour moved across it. He could only see these shadows against the darkness of the cold spot.

The man was now shouting and then another indistinct voice joined in. It was lighter and higher in tone, a woman's voice he thought. He still couldn't make out any of the words but the tenor of the voices still told a story, him threatening, her pleading. The fear inside him grew even stronger. The woman was sobbing but the man was shouting louder, his anger white hot and unstoppable. For a second his words became quite distinct.

'Kill you!' he shouted.

Martin heard a loud bang and at exactly the same time a flash of pure white light exploded, blinding him for a split second. It was so fast that he thought he might have imagined it except that the shadow of it was still on the back of his eye.

Whatever it was it was over. The room felt flat, the energy had totally gone out of it.

Martin flashed his torch over at the girls. Lydia was busy writing away in her notebook while beside her Madison was now sitting up. She was awake and wide eyed. He looked at the clock. Forty three minutes had gone. He got up and turned the lights on.

'Are you okay?' he asked the girls.

Lydia nodded and gave him a strained smile. Martin could tell that she was far from being okay but it wasn't going to stop her from writing down what she'd just witnessed.

'Madison?' Martin asked.

She looked lost and disorientated.

'Had a bad dream,' she said in a voice that might have been a little girl's.

'Write it down right now, whatever you can remember,' Martin said.

He turned to Jerzy who was replaying some of the recorded data on the screen.

'Did you feel it too?' Martin whispered.

'God, yes! That was scary but bloody fantastic,' Jerzy said shaking his head in wonder. 'Were you scared?'

'Bloody petrified if I'm honest but it was strange. It felt as though it was part of what was going on rather than my reaction to it. I don't know perhaps I'm wrong.'

'No, I know exactly what you mean. It felt like it was coming from the outside rather than from the inside,' Jerzy said.

'I hope we've got all that recorded.'

'I've checked and as far as I can see it's all there. I'm backing it all up now. For once I think we might have some really amazing data, I can't wait to start analysing it all.'

Martin had a look around the room. Nothing was out of place, it was exactly as it had been when they'd started the session. There was no bird or anything else living in the room apart from the four of them. He went near the cold spot and breathed out. The icy column was still there.

For the first time he felt a thrill of fear, his own fear this time, and his wife's words returned to him. Had he really bitten off more than he could chew with this experiment? He dismissed his fears knowing that he was going to carry on whatever happened. He had to find out what this was all about.

He had to.

Chapter Seven – Session2: Josh and Jonathan

Martin collected the notes from Lydia and Madison and then placed them in individual plastic bags with their names and the session number on it. He had to make sure that he didn't get them mixed up. He carefully sealed the bags and placed them in his briefcase. He turned back to the girls.

'Bit dramatic that, wasn't it?' Martin said.

Lydia nodded and gave him a look that made it clear that she couldn't have agreed more.

'I fell asleep, didn't I?' Madison said with a puzzled expression. 'Did I miss something?'

'Are you okay now? You looked a bit dazed when you woke up.'

'Yeah I'm okay, I just had a bad dream I suppose.'

'Do you get lots of bad dreams?' Martin asked.

'Sometimes but I can never quite remember what they were about when I wake up. I know they were bad because I wake up feeling scared or sad but then I'm okay a few minutes later. It's just a dream, isn't it?'

Martin wasn't so sure. He couldn't help thinking that Madison's late night might have done his research a real favour.

As he led the two girls downstairs Martin said, 'Oh by the way whatever happens up here can you please keep it to yourself until we finish the experiment. I don't want any ideas planted in the others' heads about what they might expect when they go up for their session.'

'Sure no problem,' Lydia said with a confirming smile.

'No problem for me,' Madison said. 'I can't remember anything anyway.'

'Now don't forget that I need you to spend as much time as it takes to write down again exactly what you saw, what you heard and what you felt up there. Madison if you can remember anything at all about your dream then please put it down on paper. After that you can have a drink and a sleep if you want. I've ordered pizzas to be delivered after we've finished the next session.'

Josh and Jonathan both stood up and looked at the three of them with great interest as they walked towards them.

'Any luck?' Josh asked with a smile. 'Anything go bump in the night up there?'

Lydia's serious expression and the sharp glance she gave Martin took the smile off Josh's face.

'Something happened up there, didn't it?' he asked looking suddenly serious.

'I can't say,' Lydia replied. 'Martin wants us to keep what happens up there to ourselves for now.'

'I don't want you going up there with any pre-conceived notions or expectations in your head,' Martin said looking at Josh and Jonathan. 'I know it might be difficult but try not to talk about it to anyone until the end of the experiment.'

'I couldn't talk about it anyway, I fell asleep,' Madison said answering a question that no-one had asked.

'You didn't?' Jonathan said with a somewhat sceptical expression.

'I did and it was my own fault. I had a bit of a late night last night and didn't get much sleep,' she replied as she looked around the room. 'I could do with a bit more too.'

Madison went to the other side of the heater where an old padded pub bench seat stood next to the wall.

'That'll do for me,' she said.

'Don't forget Madison, notes first then sleep afterwards.'

'Alright,' she said sulkily, glancing at the comfort of the bench in the same way she'd previously been eying Martin.

'Okay then Jonathan, Josh, are you ready?' Martin asked.

He could see that both of them had their notebooks, pens and torches in their hands. They said nothing as they went up the stairs but Martin could sense some trepidation in the both of them.

When they walked into the function room they both looked around as though they were expecting to see something unusual. All they saw was Jerzy standing up with his hands behind his head having a long stretch.

'Okay then, if the two of you sit at that table on the other side of Jerzy and make yourself comfortable,' Martin said. 'And remember no talking unless it's something important. You may hear Jerzy and me whispering from time to time but just try to ignore it. If it all gets too much for you just shout and I'll turn the lights on straight away. Is that clear?'

Josh gave him a quick smile. Jonathan said nothing. Martin thought that he was looking a little pale.

'Are we okay to go Jerzy?' Martin asked.

'Sure, oh and by the way I double checked that thermal imaging camera just in case and it's working fine.'

As he walked over to the light switch Martin thought back to what they'd seen when they'd heard the sound of the bird's wings and wondered what on earth could produce a visible light yet had absolutely no heat? The only thing that readily came to mind was bioluminescence. That produced a 'cold light' but it relied on some complicated chemical processes that went on inside an animal.

He turned his torch on and asked, 'Have you got your pens and notebooks at the ready and made sure that your torches are turned on?'

Josh and Jonathan both nodded.

Martin then flicked the light switch and found his way back to his seat. He turned off his torch and the room was once again plunged into darkness. He checked the screens. There was nothing. While the column of cold air was still well delineated in the thermal imaging camera Martin had no sense of the energy in the room ramping up as it had in the previous session.

He wrote on his pad, 'Feels a bit flat.'

Jerzy nodded and replied on his pad, 'Me too.'

The screens were static for the next fifteen minutes or so when the microphones started picking something up. It was so faint at first that Martin couldn't hear anything but it gradually resolved itself into something they'd heard in the previous session, two notes going from lower to higher.

Again Martin couldn't shake off the feeling that it was a child's voice asking for something but what? He listened carefully but it was so muffled that only the pitch of the two sounds could be discerned. It gradually faded away again.

There was a deep silence for the next twenty minutes or so and Martin had just about given up any hope of anything happening when he heard another sound. Even though it started off as though it was far away he could clearly make out what it said.

'Boy!'

Martin flashed his torch beam to his right. Josh gave him a look of surprise but Jonathan didn't move, he was just staring straight ahead.

'Boy, here!' the voice said.

A sudden dread and feeling of helplessness washed over Martin but it only lasted a split second and then it was gone. Nothing happened in the remaining few minutes.

At precisely forty five minutes Martin put the lights back on.

'Make sure you write down everything you heard or felt during the session and then give your notes to me.'

Martin looked at his two volunteers. Josh looked the same as he always did but Jonathan looked white and Martin could see that his hand was shaking a little as he wrote. Did the sounds they'd just heard have something to do with him?

Once they'd finished he put the notes in plastic bags with their names on and placed them in his briefcase. As he led them back downstairs he couldn't help thinking that, while this last session wasn't quite as spectacular as the first, something had definitely happened.

Martin noticed that Lydia went straight over to Jonathan and asked him if he was alright. So it wasn't just him who thought that he looked a bit shaken. He looked around for Madison. She was wrapped in her blanket and was fast asleep on the bench seat. Lydia started making coffee as Josh and Jonathan started writing their second set of notes.

Martin looked at his watch, it was one forty.

'Keep an ear open for a knock on the door. It won't be a ghostly spirit but our pizzas arriving,' Martin said with a smile.

From their reaction he couldn't help feeling that his attempt at a joke had fallen somewhat short of the mark.

Jerzy ambled down the stairs a few minutes later. Martin nodded for him to join him a little out of earshot of the rest.

'Well that really was something, prof!' Jerzy said with a smile.

'Yes, it was wasn't it? I'd have been happy with just one of those manifestations before we started. You're sure that it's all been recorded okay?'

'Yes don't worry. Just in case I've uploaded all the data into the cloud so it's absolutely safe,' Jerzy said as he looked at the subdued group. 'Do you think they're okay?'

'I hope so. I'll have a word with Jonathan before he goes up again, he looked a little pale after that session...'

Martin's words were interrupted by a banging on the door. He opened it to see a hooded figure standing outside. He was quite young and his body was half set to run away.

'Pizzas, I take it?' Martin said.

The young man in the hoodie relaxed.

'Yes four extra-large and twelve cokes. I was sure this must be the wrong address,' he said.

Martin and Jerzy helped the delivery man carry the pizzas and drinks inside. He looked around the derelict pub while Martin counted out the cash.

'What you doing in here?' the delivery man said with a puzzled expression.

'None of your business,' Martin replied as he handed him the cash.

The delivery man seemed quite reluctant to go so Jerzy herded him towards and then out of the door.

The noise and the smell of pizza woke Madison up.

'Oh good,' she said as she sat up. 'I'm starving.'

It looked like the rest were too as the group descended on the pizzas like ravenous gulls. A few minutes later only a single slice of four cheese was left. Jerzy looked at each of them before snaffling it.

Martin had been observing them closely as they ate. Josh sat a little apart from the rest. Martin suspected he was a bit like himself in that he was quite happy being in his own company, not only that but Martin suspected that he was observing the rest just as closely as he was.

Madison had taken the nearest seat and was sitting next to Jonathan. They didn't talk apart from Madison asking if Jonathan could pass the peperoni. Madison never glanced once at Jonathan but he was certainly looking at her. Martin felt a little sorry for him, he was obviously the shy type.

He also couldn't help noticing that Lydia had made sure that she got the seat next to Jerzy. He was fairly certain that his assistant was totally unaware of the fact that Lydia might be interested in him. They looked as if they'd be an odd pair, after all Jerzy looked like a giant next to her, but somehow Martin thought that his assistant had better watch out. Lydia was quite attractive, especially her eyes, and these were now firmly fixed on Jerzy. Unfortunately for his assistant he was having an animated conversation with Josh and didn't notice.

Martin managed to catch Jerzy's eye and he nodded towards the stairs. It was time to prepare for the next session.

He watched Jerzy as he made his way towards the stairs. He noticed that he wasn't the only one. Lydia had turned in her seat and had her eyes fixed on his assistant as he made his way up the stairs. He really would have to give Jerzy a heads up.

'Okay,' Martin said, 'Next up its Josh and Madison. As before don't forget your notebooks, pens and torches.'

He glanced back at Jonathan and Lydia as he made for the stairs. Lydia had her headphones on and was busily scribbling away in a notebook. Jonathan just sat there looking at them as they walked away. Martin once again felt sorry for him, at that moment he looked a lonely man.

Chapter Eight – Session 3: Josh and Madison

'Okay then it's the same drill as before,' Martin said as he watched Josh and Madison seat themselves and get their notebooks ready.

He was nearly going to ask Madison to make sure she stayed awake but then he bit his tongue. It had occurred to him that her falling asleep might have played a big part in the manifestations.

He turned towards Jerzy, 'Ready?'

'Ready as I'll ever be. I wonder if there'll be any more fireworks.'

'We can only hope,' Martin said softly with a grin before he turned back to face Josh and Madison. 'Are you both ready?' They both nodded. 'Now remember if you feel it starting to get to you just shout and I'll turn the lights back on straight away. Okay torches on.'

He turned his own on and then switched off the lights. He quickly made his way back to his seat and looked at the dashboard.

There was nothing. Over the next fifteen minutes or so there was even more of it. Martin kept checking the time on the screen imagining that whole minutes had gone by when it was no more than a few seconds. At the seventeen minute mark the microphones started picking something up. He could tell from the display that it was the strange two tone sound again and it was still going from lower to higher. The sound gradually got louder without getting any clearer and again Martin felt that he should know what it was.

'Wind effect?' Martin scrawled on his pad.

'Doubt it – keeps moving location,' Jerzy wrote back.

It gradually faded away and silence fell once again.

Nothing else happened for quite a while. The screens were blank and unmoving. Then the sound display started showing some peaks. Martin listened hard. It sounded like footsteps, footsteps coming closer but there was something else, a crunching sound. Yes that was it! It was like the sound of someone walking on broken glass. The steps came closer and he could hear a voice, it was more of a growl really. What was it saying?

Martin couldn't make anything out until the sounds became louder.

'Where are you?' the voice growled menacingly.

Martin felt a stab of fear as the steps came even closer. He looked at the computer screen, it was still only the sound display that was showing any activity. He peered into the darkness half expecting to be able to see something coming towards him but there was nothing.

The steps came even nearer and were now sounding as if they were only a matter of feet away.

'Where are you?' the voice shouted.

It made Martin jump but the second the voice had said this he knew that, whatever it was, it was over. He waited a few seconds to be sure then turned his torch on and flashed it at Josh and Madison. They looked scared but then again they had every right to be. He gave them the thumbs up and they both gave the thumbs up sign back.

He turned off the torch and waited to see if anything else happened. He looked at the clock, just twenty three minutes had passed. It seemed a hell of a lot longer.

Martin had expected to get a feeling of flatness after the last manifestation but there was still a tingling sense of expectation in the room. Over the next ten minutes or so exactly nothing happened. The seconds passed by even more slowly and he already felt as if the session had been going for hours instead of minutes. Yes there wasn't even a flicker on the computer screen.

And yet there was something though, Martin thought.

On reflection the feeling of lethargy and time slowly passing by in leaden boots seemed to be unconnected to him in some way. The feeling gradually got more intense. It actually took some effort for Martin to scrawl a message to Jerzy.

'Feel slow?'

'Yes I...'

Jerzy was about to say that he felt it too when the mics picked up a sound. It wasn't the two tone sound that they'd hear before but a monotone beeping sound. It was very faint but regular...beep...beep...beep...beep...

Martin timed it at a just over a second between each sound. Again it sounded familiar, a medical monitor perhaps?

His eye was drawn to the cold spot and the faint shadows that were now moving across it. He couldn't detect any patterns, they just looked like random flickers of light and dark. The beeping steadily got louder. The feeling of lethargy had gone, replaced by a rising feeling of dread. The fireflies were flying again. They wheeled like red sparks around the cold spot as if caught in some invisible current of air. Martin glanced over at the thermal imaging camera. There was nothing on the screen.

Martin started feeling ill and feverish, like flu but worse. He wondered if he was suddenly coming down with something but again the feeling had a strange sort of disconnect as if it too was coming from somewhere else.

The fireflies coalesced into a vague milky white blob that very gradually grew larger. Martin felt a wild fear growing inside him. As the blob got larger so did his dread of it. He glanced over at the screens. The camera was picking it all up but again the thermal imaging camera showed nothing.

The blob gradually became larger and seemed to move from side to side as it did so. The fear inside him grew and it was very close to becoming uncontrollable. He'd never felt this scared in his life before.

Martin wondered as a small voice in his head disagreed with him.

The blob was very large now but, even as it got bigger, it revealed no details. It was as if he was looking at it through a camera that was badly out of focus.

Martin clearly heard the words, 'Pay-ma, pay-ma, pay-ma!' but it was somehow as if he'd said them himself.

The white featureless blob came even closer and the fear became total and the voice became louder.

'Pay-ma, pay-ma, pay-ma, PAY-MA!'

The last two syllables had been a scream.

Then there was silence. It was over.

Martin had been holding his breath without knowing it. He released it and the fear went with it. Some rational thoughts started to percolate through his brain. The first was that he'd pissed himself. He felt his crotch but it was dry, yet the residual feeling of wetness didn't leave him. He looked at the clock. Thirty nine minutes had past. Enough was enough. He turned on his torch, found the light switch and turned it on.

He turned around and looked at Madison, her eyes were wide with fright. Josh had his head down, his hands were shaking. Even Jerzy looked white but it didn't stop him from ensuring that he got everything backed up as soon as possible. As terrible as the experience had been, he knew that he had just witnessed something historic.

Martin went over to the two students.

'Are you okay Madison? Josh?' he asked.

She nodded.

'Well I was wrong about one thing,' she said, 'it was anything but boring.'

Her attempt at a joke brought a faint smile to Josh's face.

'How about you Josh?' Martin asked.

'That was…I don't have any words,' he said.

'Are you both able to write? It's important to get what you felt down but if you're not up to it…'

Martin was interrupted by Josh, 'No, I'll be okay. You're right, this is important.'

He waited a few seconds for his hands to stop shaking and then he started writing. Madison followed suit.

Martin went over to Jerzy.

'God that was bad,' he said in a whisper.

'I know, I don't think I've ever felt so scared in my life and yet I don't think it was me that was scared but somehow I could still feel it,' Jerzy replied. 'I was so sure that I'd wet myself too but I hadn't.'

'Yes it's strange but I felt that too. What about the sounds, you know the screams, did you record all of that okay?'

'What do you mean the 'pay-ma'?'

'Yes it must have registered at quite a few decibels.'

Jerzy shook his head.

'It didn't register at all,' Jerzy said.

He replayed the last few minutes and there was silence. There were no peaks on the sound display.

'Yet you heard it too, didn't you?' Martin asked. 'Pay-ma, pay-ma, ending up with a shrill scream.'

'Yes that's exactly what I heard, except of course I couldn't have heard it because there was no sound.'

Martin was beginning to wonder if the experiment had already gone too far. He looked around the room and then directly at the point where the cold spot was. He looked down at the thermal imaging display and there it was, upright and unwavering, a column of what exactly?

Martin had no idea but he was starting to get worried. It was no longer just about sounds and images. Whatever it was had now started to directly access their minds.

Chapter Nine – Session 4: Jonathan and Lydia

Martin waited until both Josh and Madison had stopped writing before saying anything further. The feeling of fear was slipping away from him as though after a bad dream.

'Okay, if you're both finished, let's go downstairs,' he said.

They seemed only too glad to be leaving the room.

'Jerzy, I think we need to take a break before the next one. Come on down when you've finished and get yourself a coffee.'

Jerzy nodded. Something stronger might have been better, he thought, but coffee would do.

As they walked down the stairs he could feel Jonathan's and Lydia's eyes on them. They knew something had happened. He could see their expressions change. At first they looked inquisitively at them but now they looked concerned.

'Lydia. I'm sorry but I think we'll all need some coffee if you wouldn't mind,' Martin asked.

'Sure,' she replied.

'I'll help you,' Jonathan said.

'I'm sorry if I sound a bit heartless but could you both get writing again? It's really important we get it all down,' Martin said.

They both nodded and, without a word, got down to work.

Martin went over to get his coffee.

'What on earth happened up there?' Lydia whispered. 'You all came down looking like you'd seen a ghost.'

'I can't really tell you,' Martin said, 'but you're right, something did happen.'

Lydia looked up on hearing footsteps on the stairs. Jerzy slowly went down step by step. He looked very serious and thoughtful. It was not an expression that Martin had often seen on him before. He turned and looked at Lydia. Her eyes were fixed on Jerzy and they sparkled.

'Do you want a coffee?' Lydia asked Jerzy as he came towards them.

'Oh yes please. I don't suppose you've got any whisky have you?' he asked while attempting a smile.

'Sorry no,' Lydia replied.

'You mean that you haven't got a bottle somewhere in one of your boxes?' Martin said trying to keep it light. 'You surprise me.'

Madison stopped writing and felt around in her bag. She produced a half bottle of vodka and, without asking, splashed some in everyone's coffee. No-one protested.

'Thanks Madison,' Martin said.

He looked closely at her as she went back to her writing. She was turning out to be something more than he'd expected, a lot more perhaps. Once they'd both finished writing Martin collected their notes and placed them in separate plastic bags.

'You can go back to the hotel now if either of you want to,' Martin said.

They both nodded and Martin let them out.

'Get some sleep if you can and I'll see you back here at eight o'clock this evening,' Martin said, hoping that they actually would come back.

Neither said a word, they just nodded again. They both looked worn out.

'Okay then, time for the last session of the night,' Martin said as he turned to Jonathan and Lydia. He'd tried to sound light and positive but he just sounded shrill.

They both had their notebooks, pens and torches and a look of apprehension on their faces. Jerzy went up first and they all straggled up behind him.

They sat there in the dark and the silence for just over half an hour before Martin got up and turned on the lights. The room felt absolutely flat and he knew nothing was going happen. He told Lydia and Jonathan to write down what they'd felt, even if was just that they were bored.

'Anything?' Martin asked.

'Not really, that two tone sound appeared again. I could see the peaks on the sound monitor but it was too low for us to be able to hear. Apart from that there was nothing.'

'Yes it was like the previous session had sucked all the energy out of the room,' Martin said.

'You could be right there,' Jerzy replied. 'One thing I did notice was that the cold spot had gotten a few degrees warmer after the 'pay-ma' manifestation. It's gradually getting colder again but it's still nearly a degree off what it was before.'

Martin found that observation really interesting. He looked around and found that they'd both finished writing.

'When you've finished backing up and turning everything off, meet me downstairs. Once these two have gone we need to talk,' Martin said.

It didn't take long before they'd finished their second set of notes and Martin let them out. They both looked exhausted. It was raining and still dark out. He looked at his watch. It was now ten past four. He sat down and thought while he waited for Jerzy. It had been a truly crazy night. Before tonight he'd have been happy with just one small manifestation but this was way beyond anything he could have dreamt of.

While he waited he started collating all the student's notes. He first laid them all out on the table then he checked the names on the plastic bags and placed each student's notes in another bag with their name on.

While he was still doing this Jerzy came down the stairs slowly with that same thoughtful expression on his face he'd had before. He was clutching his precious laptop against his chest with both hands.

'What the fuck was that all about?' Jerzy exclaimed as he walked towards Martin.

Jerzy using a swear word almost shocked Martin. Despite his slightly dishevelled 'Viking extra cum rock guitarist' look using such a word was quite unlike him.

'I don't know but it's the strangest thing I've ever come across or even heard about if I'm honest. Are you still scared?' Martin asked.

Jerzy gave this a little thought.

'No, I don't think I am but if I had any sense I think I'd be giving upstairs a very wide berth from now on. Seriously though what's your best guess?'

It was Martin's turn to be thoughtful.

'Okay, when in your life were you the most scared?' he asked.

Jerzy's face crinkled with the effort of thinking.

'Probably just a few minutes ago I should think.'

'I remember when I was young the wardrobe used to scare me silly. It was old and it had an ornate handle that looked like a weird face in the shadows cast by the little night light I had. It used to petrify me so much that I couldn't sleep and I'd have to get up and open the wardrobe door so I couldn't see it. We forget it but sometimes when we're children we can experience fear in its sharpest and purest form. That's what the 'pay-ma' manifestation felt like to me, a child's irrational fear.'

'Yes I think I see what you're getting at,' Jerzy replied. 'Do you think that this...er...'ghost field' or whatever it is can somehow stimulate our early memories?'

'That's what I'm guessing is happening, after all if ghosts are just the shadows of people who have gone before us why should we fear them so much? It would be like projecting a film on a wall and that should scare no-one. Not only that but, people who say that they've witnessed a manifestation, often report seeing quite different things. That's always puzzled me a bit. However if this 'ghost field' somehow directly stimulates our early memories then it would all make sense and it would also explain why it terrifies us all so much. Anyway it's still just a theory at the moment but, you never know, part of the proof might be right here,' Martin said waving at the pile of notes on the table. 'By the way 'ghost field' isn't a bad term for it. Like an electrical field but much scarier. Let's call it that from now on, shall we?'

'But wouldn't people know it was their memory though?'

'Not necessarily, I'd guess that the most painful memories are those that we don't know we carry around with us. We often bury the most traumatic childhood memories so we can't access them directly but that doesn't mean that they're not there. Not only that but there's also 'childhood amnesia' to think about. This means that most people can't access memories before the age of three or four anyway. I'm just wondering if the power of the manifestation depends on the intensity of this 'ghost field'. Many ghosts are seen as shadowy or momentary phenomena and aren't often capable of being recorded whereas this...'

'Yes it's all too real and physical, isn't it? Well hopefully we've got it all on here,' Jerzy said as he stroked his laptop.

'Anyway that's probably enough thinking for one night. I've absolutely had it now and I'm ready for my bed.'

'What time are we meeting up here tomorrow?' Jerzy asked.

'I've asked everyone to be here by eight, if they all turn up that is. I certainly wouldn't blame them if they didn't. Have you noticed that the 'fireworks', as you call it, only happen when Madison's involved?' Martin asked.

'No I hadn't but you're right enough.'

'If the session with just Madison or the joint session with her and Jonathan give us more manifestations then we'll be a little more certain that it's connected to her in some way. You know people go on about 'mediums' and I'm wondering if there might be something in that. I don't mean that they really see dead people and all that but that they might have some sort of multiplying effect on the manifestation. Perhaps she can somehow tune in to the 'ghost field' better than most people. She's done a session with both Lydia and Josh now but I'm really curious to see what happens when she does one with Jonathan. Anyway if you want to go out I'll turn everything off and lock up.'

Jerzy still had that thoughtful look on his face when Martin joined him outside on the pavement. It was still dark but the streetlights looked even brighter than normal, cars and even buses passed by and some shops were still open. They started walking towards the hotel. Martin looked up at Jerzy and decided it was time for the 'heads up'.

'By the way Lydia really fancies you.'

Jerzy stopped dead and gave Martin a look of surprise.

'No she doesn't, does she?'

'Yes she does, although God knows why,' Martin replied trying to keep a straight face.

Jerzy started walking and then stopped again.

'No she doesn't, does she?' he repeated.

This time the stress was on the 'does she?' He clearly still didn't believe Martin.

'Look I am a psychologist and so I should know about these things but to be honest even if I wasn't I'd know. All you need to do is see the way she looks at you. So what do you think?'

'What do I think? I mean she's gorgeous, I mean really gorgeous. I noticed that the first second I saw her but I never thought, I mean...she doesn't, does she?' he said with a sort of half hopeful smile.

'Yes she does. For God's sake have a word with her yourself tomorrow will you?'

'I will,' Jerzy said with a sloppy smile.

Before they went to their rooms they agreed to meet up in Jerzy's room at six to have a quick look at the data.

Martin climbed into bed, set his alarm for four thirty that afternoon and lay back in an attempt to go to sleep. He thought he'd have trouble but in a matter of seconds he was in a deep sleep. He didn't remember dreaming although he had to admit that any dream he might have had couldn't have been weirder than what he'd just witnessed in the Black Vaults.

Chapter Ten – The start of the second night

Martin was still deeply asleep when his alarm went off. He turned it off and lay back for a while. He was still only half awake as the memories of the previous night slowly trickled back into his consciousness. At first he was sure that he must be remembering a weird dream that he'd just had. He sat up sharply when the realisation hit him that these were real memories and not dreams.

Half a day later the events of the night before seemed even stranger and more improbable than they had at the time. He couldn't help smiling though. He'd come to the Black Vaults to get some evidence to support his theories and it looked like he was getting it by the bucket load. He had a sudden thrill of fear as he thought of the possibility that the data might have been lost somehow. He trusted Jerzy but the niggling thought just wouldn't go away. So he showered and dressed and went to Jerzy's room.

He tapped softly on the door and Jerzy opened it. He too was fully dressed.

'I thought it might be you. Don't worry all the data's still there and it's all backed up. I was up at three and that was the first thing I checked.'

'When I first woke up I thought it was just a strange dream I'd had,' Martin said.

Jerzy pointed towards the laptop. A video was playing. It showed a stream of bright red sparks coalesce into a white blob.

'If I'm honest that's a big relief and you're right, I was worried that the data might have been lost,' Martin said. 'This is important Jerzy, perhaps the most important thing that will ever happen to us.'

It was strange watching the white blob grow bigger on the screen. Without the sense of dread and 'pay-ma' screaming in his head it looked quite bland.

'Have you started any sort of analysis yet?' Martin asked.

Jerzy shook his head.

'I've just been making sure that it's all there. I don't want to start any analysis until we've finished all the sessions and I know what I'm up against.'

'Fair enough,' Martin replied.

In truth he was itching to find out more about what they'd witnessed but he also knew that he'd have to be patient. He reminded himself that he was a scientist and that they'd decided on how they were going to carry out the analysis long before they'd arrived at the Black Vaults. He knew that they'd have to stick to the meticulous methodology that they'd agreed on if they were going to get a paper out of it. It still didn't stop him itching though.

'Was that true, you know what you said last night?' Jerzy asked in a sort of sideways fashion.

Martin knew what he was asking about and decided to have a bit of fun before answering.

'Oh absolutely,' Martin replied. On seeing Jerzy smile he continued, 'Yes I really think it could well be something to do with childhood memories.'

Jerzy's smile disappeared.

'No I meant, well, you know?'

'You're being a bit non-specific there,' Martin observed. He decided to put his friend out of his obvious misery. 'I take you're referring to the lovely Lydia?'

'Yes, yes what you said about Lydia. Was that true?'

'Yes it was. I wouldn't pull your leg about something as serious as that now would I?' Martin said.

'No I'd guess you wouldn't, would you?'

The 'would you' ended up as a real question.

'No really I wouldn't. All I can say is have a word with her yourself if you can tonight and please do it as soon as possible. I need that massive brain of yours to be concentrating on the job in hand. Now on to another, incredibly valuable piece of research I carried out before we came here.'

'Oh what's that?' Jerzy asked.

'There's a pub not more than ten minutes walk from here that does an all day brunch; eggs, bacon, sausage, beans and chips. Interested?'

'Oh I should say so,' Jerzy said with some enthusiasm. 'I'm absolutely starving.'

Josh woke when his alarm went off. It was nearly six. He couldn't think for a moment but he was fairly sure that he'd set it for four o'clock. He'd wanted to get some research done before going to the pub. He sat up and rubbed his face with his hands. He still felt exhausted. He hadn't slept well. When he wasn't thinking about last night he seemed to be dreaming about it. Well one bit of last night anyway.

While he was showering the vague memory of getting woken up by the alarm and feeling so tired that he moved it forward by two hours came back to him. For some reason this made him feel a bit better. Some of the cobwebs in his head were also washed away while he showered. After he dried himself he sat naked on the bed for a while trying to gather his thoughts.

That last session with Madison was what he'd been thinking about. The phantom steps and growling voice that had started off the session had been freaky enough but that white blob and the word 'pay-ma' were far worse. He felt that it should mean something to him but he couldn't think what it was. The fear and dread he felt as the apparition came closer felt like it was coming from inside him. Then he remembered the most shameful part of the previous night.

He'd pissed himself.

He felt a deep shame, he'd never done anything like that in his life, well not since he'd been a kid. Luckily for him he'd had his parka on and that covered up his wet jeans. As they were the only jeans he had with him he'd left them near the heater all night. He went over and checked them and thankfully they were dry. He brought the crotch area up to his nose and smelt it. There was still a faint smell of urine. He'd have to go heavy on the deodorant tonight.

He glanced at the clock and found that it was now a quarter to seven. He sprayed himself liberally and then sprayed the crotch of his jeans. He quickly dressed himself. His stomach rumbled and he realised that he was hungry. He remembered that there was a burger place not too far away. He'd go there. It wouldn't be the first time that he'd had a burger and fries for breakfast.

She lay awake for a few minutes thinking over what had happened. The last session had been a bit boring but in a way she wasn't disappointed. She was more than glad that it hadn't been as eventful as the one with Josh and Madison. She still didn't know what had happened but, from the look on their faces, she knew that it must have been something really bad.

Then she thought about Jerzy and smiled. She still couldn't quite figure out why she felt such an attraction to him. It was totally unlike her. Long before she went to university she'd decided that she was going to concentrate on her studies and that she wouldn't indulge herself by having any romances on the side. There would be plenty of time for that afterwards she'd told herself.

She'd been able to stick to this plan with ease, there'd been a few boys who had tried, oh yes and one girl now she remembered, but she'd made it absolutely clear to all of them that she wasn't interested. So what was it about Jerzy that had so instantly changed her mind?

She'd always been attracted to intelligent people, that much she knew, and Jerzy was certainly in that category but there was more to it than that. Plato suddenly came to mind and his tale of humans originally having four arms, four legs and two faces. However the Gods had created such perfection that they became jealous of their own creation and so they split each of them into two parts, each having just half a soul each. And so forever afterwards each person's life is spent in searching for the other half of their soul.

She smiled. She knew that she was being over-romantic as usual but she also knew that there was something of that in how she felt about Jerzy. It was as if they'd met somewhere before and had understood each other then.

'Come on you daft radge and get on with it,' she said out loud in an effort to rouse herself to action.

For some reason when she talked to herself it was always in a strident Edinburgh accent.

'Well no point in being mad if you don't show it,' she added with a smile.

While she showered her spirits dropped somewhat. While she knew she liked Jerzy and she thought she'd made it quite obvious, it occurred to her that he hadn't really responded in the same way. She'd noticed him looking at her from time to time but that might just be because he thought she was weird or something. Doubts began to creep into her mind.

Was she just imagining it after all? she wondered.

She hoped not. Yet she knew that, for all of her stark black clothes and business-like demeanour, she was really an incurable romantic. After all she had brought a Jane Austen with her to read before she went to sleep.

She looked at herself in the mirror and frowned. She rummaged around in her back pack and found a red and gold silk scarf that she'd brought along without really knowing why. She put on some make up and wrapped the scarf around her neck and surveyed herself in the mirror again. It definitely looked better. She wished herself luck.

She wondered if there'd be any more fireworks tonight during the sessions. However she knew that the only fireworks that she really wanted to see happen were between her and Jerzy.

She woke up curled into a tight foetal ball. She'd had another bad dream. As usual she was never quite sure what the dream had been about except for the fact that it had been dark and nasty. She blearily looked over at the clock. It was nearly six. She somehow found the energy to sit up. She didn't move for some minutes as she wondered what she should do next.

After what had happened she knew that no-one would blame her if she didn't turn up for the second night. The thought of going back to sleep was seductive until she remembered the dream and concluded that maybe that wasn't such a good idea after all. She sat on the edge of her bed hugging herself with no clear idea of what to do next. She could see herself in the mirror.

Her front of being a girly-girl who was only interested in partying and sex was just that. Behind that thin veneer was someone who had a large hole in her life, a black hole at that. She felt sad and sometimes almost suicidal but without truly ever knowing why. All the drinking and clubbing and shagging were just at attempt to distract herself from thinking. Thinking inevitably made her feel even worse and here she was doing it again.

She roused herself and climbed into the shower. While she let the water run down her body she decided that she might as well go back to the pub for the second night. It would be better than being alone anyway.

He was awake exactly two minutes before the alarm was due to go off. He got straight up and into the shower. While he let the water wash the sleep away he thought about the night before. His sessions had obviously not been as eventful as some but there was one moment that was still stuck in his head.

When he'd been sitting next to Josh a voice had shouted 'Boy!'

He knew that it was something to do with him, something that was in a box in his mind marked 'Do not open' in big red letters. He'd felt an immediate fear and knew who the voice belonged to yet he couldn't put a name to it. In order to do that he'd have to open the box.

After drying himself he sat on the bed and wondered whether he should just get the train back home. The word 'home' however struck him as being totally inappropriate. As nice as his flat was it definitely wasn't that. In truth it was cold and lonely. He realised that the only other person other than himself who had set foot in that flat was his father who had come to look it over when he'd first rented it.

He should write a book, he thought, 'How to Be Excruciatingly Lonely While Studying with Ten Thousand Other People'. It was really quite a feat.

He decided he'd go to the pub and keep his promise to the professor. He might be scared silly but at least he wouldn't be alone.

Chapter Eleven – In the Black Vaults again

Martin opened the padlock on the steel door and walked into the darkness. He switched on the power and the bar was illuminated. Nothing had changed. The huge semi-circular bar was still ghostly looking and covered in a thick layer of white dust and the chairs were just where they'd left them this morning. He heard a soft wailing as the heater came on.

He followed Jerzy upstairs and turned the heater on there too. While Jerzy was plugging his laptop in and turning all his equipment on Martin wandered down the far end of the room. He didn't need the camera to know that the cold spot was still there as the hairs on the back of his neck were standing up. None the less he stopped and breathed out when he reached the spot. His breath was icy white.

He went back and sat by Jerzy who was rattling away at his keyboard. A few minutes later the screen showed the dashboard display. Martin's eyes went straight to the output from the thermal imaging camera. The cold spot was starkly displayed, a solid column reaching from floor to ceiling.

'What's the temperature now?' Martin asked.

'Just over minus thirteen, that's slightly colder than yesterday,' Jerzy replied. 'It looks like it's recharged itself somehow. So remind me, what's the plan of action for tonight?'

'I thought we'd do seven in all. We'll do each of them by themselves first, then Josh and Lydia and lastly it will be Jonathan and Madison together.'

'Any particular reason why they're last?'

'If I'm honest I'm not quite sure. Perhaps I'm keeping the best until last. Madison's already done one with Lydia and with Josh and, while they've been pretty spectacular, I've got a feeling that this one with Jonathan might be a bit special for some reason. Anyway they're not exactly last as we'll need to do a control session with just you and me present.'

'Okay that sounds like a plan,' Jerzy said. 'I must admit that I can't wait for it to be over.'

'You're not looking forward to tonight then?' Martin asked in some surprise.

'No it's not that, I just can't wait to start properly analysing this stuff. It would be great if we could make some sense of it all.'

'Well I'm with you there. We'll have our work cut out though. I'll ask everyone not to talk about what's happened here if they can but it will inevitably leak out before long. We'll need to get our paper and the evidence out there as soon as possible.'

'Our paper?' Jerzy asked.

'Of course 'Paranormal activity identified as a response to the stimulation of repressed childhood memories and infantile amnesia by M. Jorgensen and J. Kowalski'. How does that sound?'

'Is that going to be the title?'

'I've absolutely no idea if I'm honest but it doesn't sound bad does it?'

'Thanks prof, I wasn't sure if you were going to name me as an author. After all I'm just a grad assistant.'

Martin looked around the room at all the equipment that Jerzy had put together. He knew how long it had taken to build and what a struggle it had been just to get all the equipment in the first place.

'If I'm honest the only qualm I had was whether your name should go first but then I thought, as I'm older and uglier, why not pull rank? I suppose we could always do it in alphabetical order?'

This made Jerzy laugh as Martin would still be first anyway.

'Seriously thanks prof,' Jerzy said.

Martin looked at his watch. It was seven thirty.

'I'll put the kettle on. Come downstairs when you're ready. I just hope someone turns up or it might be just one long control session tonight.'

He could hear someone knocking on the door as he came down the stairs.

Ten to one it's Lydia, he thought as he opened the door.

'Good evening Lydia,' he said as he stepped to one side and held the door open for her.

'Oh, it's you Professor,' she replied looking slightly disappointed.

She was about to say something but Martin beat her to it.

'He's upstairs if you want to go and say hello.'

'Oh...er...okay. I'll go and do that then,' she said with some hesitation.

'Here bring him a coffee. I'll do one for you too.'

He watched her as she walked up the stairs and smiled. The splash of colour provided by her scarf hadn't gone unnoticed. He thought that it suited her. She looked quite serious and more than a little nervous. Martin could smile because he knew she had no need to be.

Jerzy was checking the wiring to one of the phones when she walked in.

'Hi, I've brought up some coffee,' she said.

'Hi...er...thanks,' Jerzy said.

An awkward silence reigned for a while.

'So how did you get into this?' Lydia asked, thankful that she could think of something to get the conversation going.

'What working with the prof? Well my mum really wanted me to be a doctor when I was a kid but she settled for me getting a job writing code when she saw that I was good with computers. So that's what I did when I first went to university, write code. In a way I suppose mum was just happy that I was going to university at all, I'm the first in our family see.'

'What about your dad?' Lydia asked.

'Dad? Oh he was fine with whatever I wanted to do. He was great in that way. He never pressured me once about getting a career that was definitely mum's job. He's a plumber by the way, yes a Polish plumber,' Jerzy said with a fond smile. 'Anyway the software engineering course was good, it was stuff I needed to know but it was, well, boring too if I'm honest. I'd figured out most of what they had to teach in the first year so I was actually thinking of quitting and going straight into a job when I attended one of Martin's classes.'

Lydia pulled a puzzled face as she asked, 'If you were on a computer course how come you tried out a psychology lecture?'

'Well if I'm honest there was this girl I liked who was on the psychology course...' Jerzy said looking somewhat embarrassed.

'What happened there?' Lydia asked, holding her breath.

'I don't think she even knew I existed,' Jerzy replied.

Jerzy didn't hear Lydia whisper the word 'good' under her breath.

'Anyway I must admit that I got quite intrigued and attended another one. After that one I got totally hooked and so I asked to switch courses and that was that. What about you? How did you land up on a psychology course?'

She looked upwards as she thought and so, for the first time, Jerzy felt able to sneak a good look at her. The profile of her face was quite beautiful he thought but it was her eyes that made him hold his breath. They were large and dark and lustrous and Jerzy thought he could detect real sadness in them. He suddenly wanted to scoop her up in his arms and protect her in some way.

When Lydia had thought of what she was going to say she moved her gaze back downwards. Their eyes met and locked. They looked unflinchingly into each other's eyes for what seemed an eternity before they both looked away with an embarrassed smile. In that split second they both knew that something had happened.

Lydia cleared her throat to disguise her breathlessness before replying, 'Well I always wanted to find out more about what goes on in people's heads, that's what comes from having a mad mum I suppose.'

'Really?' Jerzy asked.

'Oh yes, bipolar and a religious fanatic too, it's not a good combination believe me. When I was twelve she finally got sectioned so it was just me and dad. It was such a relief if I'm honest and that's something I've felt guilty about ever since. It must have been even more of a relief for poor old dad. He came in for the brunt of it unfortunately but I never heard him complain once. He must have loved her very much to have put up with her for so long, he was heartbroken when she died.'

'I'm sorry to hear that,' Jerzy said softly.

'She hung herself, no it's hanged, isn't it? Anyway she committed suicide when I was fourteen, something the two of us have been trying to deal with ever since.'

Jerzy couldn't help taking her hand in his. She looked at him and smiled a sad smile as her hand gripped his tightly.

'So anyway I suppose that's why I wanted to do psychology, to try and understand what happened, what she went through. As for this, if I'm honest, I thought it might be fun but it's...well it's not quite what I expected.'

As she said this her eyes went up and met his again. He suddenly felt as if his heartbeat had suddenly become irregular. At that moment he would have given her anything she'd have asked for. They walked back down the room and Jerzy sat down and looked at his laptop. The phone was connected now. Jerzy was silent for a moment while he plucked his courage up. His stomach flipped over several times but he just about managed to get the words out.

'Can I ask you something? You know, when this is over could we...?'

He got no further.

'Yes, yes we could,' she said.

'Good,' Jerzy replied with a wide smile.

Before he had time to change his mind she put her arms around his neck and gave him an intense kiss full on the lips.

'See you later then,' she said.

Jerzy didn't answer, he didn't need to. His big sloppy smile said it all.

Martin watched her as she came down. He smiled at seeing her looking so happy. He thought of Liz and he suddenly missed her terribly and wondered what she was doing.

Another knock on the door brought him back to the here and now. It was Josh. He looked tired.

'Want a coffee?' Martin asked.

'Sure,' Josh replied with no enthusiasm whatsoever.

He got out his notebook and started writing. He obviously wasn't up for any conversation so Martin gave him his coffee and let him be.

'So what's happening tonight?' Lydia asked.

'We'll be doing some individual sessions and then you and Josh together and the last one will be with Jonathan and Madison,' Martin replied.

'I don't mind being the last one,' she said.

I bet you don't, Martin thought. In fact when he thought about it he couldn't see any harm in it.

'Okay then, it will give the others a chance to finish a little earlier that way.'

He looked at his watch. It was one minute to eight. He went over to the door and waited. At exactly eight o'clock he heard a knock and opened the door.

'Hello, Jonathan,' he said.

It was indeed Jonathan and exactly on time as usual. Madison was also there waiting behind him. It was clear that they hadn't come together though.

'Oh and you too Madison,' he quickly added. 'Get yourselves a coffee.'

That meant that everyone had turned up. Martin found that he was mildly surprised by the fact.

Martin looked at his little group. Lydia was busying herself making coffee while Madison and Jonathan seated themselves at opposite ends of the table. Josh had just about looked up when they sat down but that was all. He couldn't help noticing a distinct change when compared to how they'd been yesterday. They all looked tired and a bit dejected, except for Lydia of course, who was like a little ray of sunshine alongside the others.

'Okay it will hopefully be a shorter night tonight for most of you although we'll be doing more sessions. That's because we don't have to spend time setting up the equipment,' Martin said. 'We'll be mostly doing individual sessions and just the two sessions with two people tonight. So perhaps we can start with Jonathan, then Madison, then Josh. Next we'll have Madison and Jonathan together and then Josh and Lydia. Last up will be Lydia on her own.'

'Why is Lydia last?' Madison asked.

Martin and Lydia looked at each other.

'Because...because she's volunteered to help Jerzy pack up his equipment,' Martin said, thinking quickly. 'Anyway it will mean that the rest of you can get off a bit earlier.'

Josh looked up, 'Aren't you going to do a control session?'

'Yes, yes we are. The very last session will be just me and Jerzy. Okay then so when you've finished your last session and written up both sets of notes you'll be free to go back to the hotel.'

'What happens after that?' Jonathan asked.

'Good question. Jerzy will be doing a detailed analysis of the digital data while I'll be doing a full textual analysis of all your notes. Once we've done that we'll marry up both analyses and then see what it tells us. I'll be carrying out some further interviews with each of you, so long as you're up for it that is, to try and clarify anything that we may have found. Is that okay?'

They all nodded.

'Okay then pizzas have been ordered for one o'clock so that should be just after Madison and Jonathan's session. By the way your rooms at the hotel are booked until the day after tomorrow so if you want a very long lie in then that's okay. Anything else?'

They all looked at him blankly.

'No? Okay then, talk amongst yourselves for a while and I'll just go and see where Jerzy's up to.'

Half way up the stairs he looked down at his little band of volunteers. They each sat apart from each other. Jonathan and Madison were gloomily looking into their coffees while Josh was busy scribbling away in his notebook. Lydia sat with a quiet smile on her face looking very much like the odd one out.

Jerzy had a similar smile on his face when Martin walked in.

'It went well then?' Martin asked.

'Oh yes, she's agreed to go out with me after we're finished here.' Jerzy's face then crinkled in puzzlement. 'Well at least I think she did. She never let me quite finish what I was going to say.'

'I wouldn't worry about that. She's offered to be last up so she can help you pack your stuff away.'

Jerzy's smile widened.

'Oh fantastic....er...I mean I could do with the help...yes that's what I meant, the help.'

'Good then I take it that it would be okay if I review the notes downstairs while you and Lydia pack everything away up here?'

'Yes, yes I'd say that sounds like an excellent idea.'

Martin smiled at seeing his assistant so smitten. He was glad though, he had the feeling that Lydia might be just what he needed.

He looked at his watch. He figured that if they started the first one at nine with a short break in between then the first four sessions should be finished before the pizzas arrived at one.

'Will you be okay if we start around nine?' Martin asked.

'Yes no problem here.'

'Will you need any help before then?'

'No, everything's up and running. I'm just doing some extra checks just in case,' Jerzy replied.

'Good I'll go and join the merry bunch downstairs and see if I can cheer them up a bit.'

Martin had half an hour or more to fill and he made his mind up what to do with it as he made his way down the stairs. He looked down and saw them all seated apart wrapped up in their own thoughts. He decided to get them talking. He sat down and everyone looked at him.

'You're all very quiet this evening,' he said. 'Tell me, how are you all feeling after last night?'

Martin looked at Lydia first, being fairly sure that he'd get a positive answer.

'I'm feeling fine, in fact never better,' she replied chirpily.

The other three looked at her in some puzzlement. Martin looked at Josh.

'A bit tired if I'm honest. I didn't sleep all that well last night. For some reason that session with Madison rocked me a bit. I couldn't get it out of my head but I've absolutely no idea why.'

'Jonathan?' Martin asked.

'I'm okay,' he replied a little nervously. 'Nothing much happened after all, did it?'

'Madison?'

She gave herself a little time to think first.

'Like Josh I'm a bit tired. I'm finding it all a bit mind-numbing to be honest, it's as if my brain's been overloaded. I want to go on with it but I just hope it's a little less exciting tonight.'

Martin could understand why she might feel like that but personally he was hoping for more fireworks.

'Okay have a serious think about it anyway and if you don't feel that you want to carry on then please let me know. Believe me there'll be no disgrace if you do.'

They all looked at each other but no-one said anything. Martin looked at his watch.

'Okay then as you're all raring to go we've got just twenty five minutes before we start with Jonathan.'

Jonathan nodded but said nothing. He could tell that they weren't exactly looking forward to it.

'Can I just say thanks to all of you for turning up tonight. I must admit that after what happened last night I had my doubts that you would. You're a really brave bunch and I just want to emphasise that we're doing something really important here, something that could be truly ground breaking so hang in there if you can. Okay I'll go up and check with Jerzy to make sure he's got everything ready and Jonathan I'll give you a shout in a bit.'

He looked back at his little group as he climbed the stairs. They'd all gone quiet and back into their shells again. He looked over at Jerzy as he walked into the room and he knew that something was wrong from his face.

'What's up?' he asked.

'Well nothing really I suppose,' he replied.

'That's not what your face is telling me.'

'It's just, I don't know, unusual I suppose.'

'Even more unusual than what we've seen so far you mean?' Martin asked with some scepticism.

'Here look,' Jerzy said as he pointed at the screen.

Martin looked. He wasn't sure what he was supposed to be seeing until Jerzy pointed at the temperature. The column was veering between minus thirteen to minus fifteen degrees in a sort of slow pulse.

'What do you think that means?' Martin asked.

'I'm not sure but I kind of get the feeling that it's pumping itself up for something.'

Martin grinned.

'Let's hope so.'

As far as Martin was concerned the more fireworks the better.

Chapter Twelve – Session 5: Jonathan

Just before nine Martin went halfway down the stairs and called Jonathan's name. He looked nervously over at the other three before he slowly followed Martin upstairs.

'You've got your torch on and your notebook ready?' Martin asked as Jonathan took his seat next to Jerzy.

Jonathan nodded without any enthusiasm. Martin could see that he was somewhat scared and he could understand that. He felt a little scared himself.

Martin turned the lights off and made his way to his seat. He looked intently at the display but nothing was happening, nothing that is apart from the strange oscillation in the temperature of the cold spot. The column was now veering between minus fourteen to minus sixteen degrees. So it's a little colder than it was before. Martin wished he knew what this meant.

They sat there in total silence for almost half an hour before Jerzy noticed the two tone sound registering on his display. It was still so low that it couldn't be heard.

'We've had this every session so far,' Jerzy wrote on his notepad.

Martin took this in but he had no idea what it meant. The two tone peaks just about came into the hearing range before gradually disappearing from the screen. Exactly nothing happened for the next five minutes or so.

Then the whispering started.

At first he wasn't sure whether he was imagining it or if it was just the wind until Jerzy stabbed his finger at the sound display. A number of peaks rose and fell in quick succession.

'It's moving around the room,' Jerzy wrote.

Martin watched as the peaks gradually grew. He could hear it now. It sounded as if several people were whispering at once so that the sounds overlapped into a sibilant jumble. Only now and again could he make out some words.

'Where, where, where?' one whisper said as if it was in an echo chamber.

'Find you, find you, find you,' another whisper said before it was drowned in the background noise that was growing by the second.

The whispering suddenly stopped and Martin felt a sense of dread overtake him. He looked at the display. It was absolutely still, absolutely nothing was happening. Yet the dreadful fear still intensified in him. He looked towards the cold spot. There was nothing but blackness. Then, in the corner of his eye, he saw something moving. It was the sound display starting to show some small peaks. The whispering started again and it seemed more strident and more urgent than before.

Again he heard the word 'Where?' as a question in the growing maelstrom of whispers.

'Where?'

Something was looking for him, something evil.

'Where?'

It was getting closer and closer.

'Where?'

The sound grew into a roar and came together in a single spoken word that was shouted by what seemed like dozens of voices.

'BOY!'

The lights went on.

Martin felt dazed and looked over towards the light switch. Jonathan was standing by it. He looked white and shaken.

'I'm sorry, I'm sorry,' he said.

Martin took a second to pull himself together. He looked over at Jerzy.

'Are you okay?' he whispered.

Jerzy was a little white but he just nodded. He was already intent on backing up all the data from the session. Martin looked at the time. The session only had two minutes to run anyway.

Martin went over to Jonathan.

'I'm sorry,' Jonathan said again.

'Why are you sorry?'

'I just couldn't stand it anymore, the whispering I mean.'

Martin thought that he looked on the verge of tears.

'It's okay Jonathan, really. All you had to do was shout and I would have turned the lights on straight away.'

'I couldn't speak, I tried but I couldn't get anything out.'

Martin quickly went over to Jerzy.

'I'll have to get Jonathan downstairs and get a coffee in him. I'll pop up later.'

'Sure,' Jerzy replied without looking up.

He led Jonathan down the stairs like he would a small child. The other three looked up at them with some concern.

'Lydia, do you think we could we have some coffee please?' Martin asked as they reached the foot of the stairs.

'Yes sure,' Lydia replied as she made herself busy.

Josh and Madison just looked on not knowing what to do.

Martin led Jonathan to a seat. Some of the colour was already returning to his cheeks.

'Are you okay?' Martin asked.

'Yes, yes I'm feeling a little better. I'm sorry about that, I'm afraid that it all just got a bit too much for me,' Jonathan replied looking somewhat embarrassed.

'Don't be sorry, I'm amazed you stuck it as long as you did and even more so that you were able to turn on the lights. I felt like I was frozen to the spot,' Martin said.

Lydia brought a cup over and gave it to Jonathan. He gave her a grateful smile.

'What happened?' Josh asked with some concern.

'Oh nothing really,' Jonathan said. 'I just had a strange feeling that's all.'

Josh didn't seem to quite believe him.

Martin took Lydia to one side.

'I'm sorry to give you the responsibility but can you look after Jonathan for a while. He's had quite a shock. I need to go up and see Jerzy.'

'Sure,' Lydia replied. 'No problem, Professor.'

He was grateful that she didn't ask any further questions. Lydia was going up in his estimation all the time.

He bounded back up the stairs to see Jerzy banging away at his keyboard. He looked worried.

'Did you get everything?' Martin asked afraid that something had gone wrong and the data was lost.

'Oh that? Yes of course. It was the first thing I checked.'

Martin gave a sigh of relief.

'What's the problem then?'

'I'm trying to figure out where the sounds were coming from. In the end it was from just about everywhere in the room but I've been able to figure out more or less exactly where that final sound came from.'

'Where was that?'

'Exactly where the cold spot is.'

'That final sound, the word 'Boy', we heard that before when Jonathan was up here didn't we?' Martin asked.

'Yes I think you're right there. It was when he was with Josh, if I remember correctly.'

'God there's so much going on here but what does it all mean?' Martin asked in some frustration as he looked down the room towards the cold spot.

Jerzy gave him a look that told him he should be patient.

'I know, we're scientists and we wait for the full analysis,' Martin said in replying to his own question. 'You know I told them downstairs that what we were doing is ground breaking. I was trying to cheer them up but it's occurring to me that I just might have been right.'

Chapter Thirteen – Session 6: Madison

Madison looked quite serious as she walked up the stairs. The sex-mad party girl persona had completely disappeared and Martin wondered if he was at last seeing something of the real Madison. He knew that she was intelligent enough from her course work it was just consistency and application that she lacked.

He noticed that she'd sensibly put some leggings on tonight but she still brought the blanket with her and draped it over her legs when she sat down. He checked that she had her torch on and her notepad ready before he looked over at Jerzy. Jerzy gave him the thumbs up and he turned off the lights and returned to his seat.

The cold spot was still changing temperature although Martin noticed that it had gotten a degree or so warmer. He wondered if that was due to Jonathan's session. All the other displays were flat. To Martin's annoyance they stayed that way for what seemed like an eternity. He watched the clock as the seconds crawled by. It felt like something was about to happen but it never did, not until the clock read thirty two minutes and twelve seconds anyway. The cold spot had gotten colder by a degree or so.

The sound display started gently pulsing. It was the sound of steps and they were coming closer. The peaks on the graph grew and the sound of someone's feet crunching on broken glass could be clearly heard. In his head a sing song voice started chanting a rhyme...

Janey and Johnny, sitting in a tree,
K-I-S-S-I-N-G
First comes love, then comes marriage
Then comes Janey with a baby carriage

As much as he tried to block the singing in his mind he couldn't. As the footsteps got closer the cadence of the rhyme became faster and the gap between each round of the rhyme became non-existent. It began to feel more like a prayer than anything else.

The footsteps were very close now and the words were being chanted so fast that they became a blur. Then the footsteps started to recede and the chanting slowed down. Slowly both sounds disappeared.

Martin looked at the clock. Only two minutes had elapsed since hearing the footsteps. It had seemed far longer. He turned on his torch and checked on Madison.

She looked back at him with frightened eyes but she tried to smile and gave him a nod.

Brave girl, Martin thought.

The rest of the session was uneventful except for the two tone sound briefly appearing briefly on the screen once again in the last minute of the session. At exactly forty five minutes Martin turned on the lights.

'Are you okay Madison?' Martin asked.

She nodded and started writing her notes.

Martin felt like looking over her shoulder to see what she was writing. Instead he turned to Jerzy.

'Everything uploaded and okay?' he asked.

'Yes, no problems there.' Then, in a near whisper, Jerzy said 'We've got another repetition here haven't we? The footsteps I mean.'

'Yes that's right. We heard the same thing when she was up here before,' Martin whispered back. 'I didn't get quite the same feeling of fear though. Did you hear that rhyme?'

'Janey and Johnny, sitting in a tree. Yes it's still going around my head now,' Jerzy replied.

'I had the feeling that it was almost like some sort of charm and so long as you keep repeating it then you'll be okay. It's the sort of thing kids do.'

'Yes that sounds about right to me,' Jerzy said as he went back to work. 'You couldn't bring a coffee with you when you come back up, could you?'

'I think I might be able to do a bit better than that,' Martin replied with a smile.

He looked at the displays while he waited for Madison to finish her notes. He found his eyes automatically drawn towards the thermal imaging screen and the hard-edged unwavering column it displayed. He noticed that it had gotten slightly colder and wondered once again what it might mean. He had the thought that, as the column got colder, it was somehow storing more energy or whatever you might call the 'stuff' that powered the 'ghost field'. He knew it broke all the laws of thermodynamics but he still thought that he might be on to something.

His thoughts were interrupted by Madison.

'I'm finished Professor,' she said as she offered him her notes.

He thanked her and carefully stowed them away in the briefcase.

'Are you really okay?' Martin asked as they walked towards the door.

'Yes, it was a bit scary but there's just the one more session to go and then it's over, isn't it?' she said.

'Yes, there's just the one more to go for you.'

Martin was really struck once again by the change in Madison. She definitely wasn't the same person he'd invited. He found himself itching to get at all the students' notes. He was desperate to find out what was behind all of this.

Chapter Fourteen – Session 7: Josh

Martin followed Madison down the stairs and the other three looked steadily at their faces as they descended trying to decipher how the session went. He went straight over to Lydia.

'I think Jerzy could do with a coffee,' Martin said.

She flashed him a smile.

'I'll bring it up if you like,' she said as she started boiling the kettle. 'How about you?'

'Oh yes please,' Martin said as he glanced over at Madison.

She was seated quietly in the corner writing up her second set of notes. Josh was also hunched over his notepad. Martin wondered what he was writing about.

'Ready for your session?' he asked.

Josh's head came up. It was quite obvious from his expression that he wasn't looking forward to it. He didn't say anything, he just nodded and returned to his writing.

'Here you go Professor,' Lydia said as she gave him a coffee.

He watched her as she walked up the stairs. He'd give her and Jerzy a few minutes before he interrupted them. With Madison and Josh writing away there was only Jonathan to talk to. He was sitting at the far end of the table by himself. He looked far from comfortable.

'How are you Jonathan?' Martin asked.

'Oh, I'm okay I suppose,' he replied.

Martin thought that his expression and body language somewhat contradicted his words.

'Just the one to go now,' Martin said trying to be positive.

Jonathan smiled a thin smile and nodded.

Martin gave up on his attempts to start a conversation and sat there quietly drinking his coffee and thinking. He looked at his watch. He'd given Jerzy and Lydia ten minutes. It was time for the next session.

'Josh, are you ready?' he asked.

Josh nodded and turned a shade paler. He stood up and made his way upstairs. Martin couldn't help noticing that he walked up the stairs as if he was walking to his own execution. His former excitement at being involved in the project had obviously evaporated somewhat. Martin walked past him and stopped just outside the door.

'Hopefully Jerzy will be ready for us,' Martin said cheerfully and a little louder than was strictly required.

He was giving Jerzy warning that he and Lydia were about to be interrupted. His warning worked as Lydia was already making her way towards the door as they walked in. Martin couldn't help noticing the smile on her face and the much sloppier one that decorated Jerzy's face.

Well at least one good thing will have come out of all this, Martin thought.

While Josh was seating himself Martin looked at the displays. The column's temperature had stopped pulsating. It was the coldest it had been yet. If Martin's guess was right he felt that the fireworks he'd been hoping for wouldn't be too far away.

'Torch on?' Martin asked.

It being Josh he didn't bother asking about the notepad.

Martin turned off the light and waited.

And waited.

Nothing happened, well almost nothing. The two tone sound kept its record of appearing at every session. Again the familiarity of it struck Martin but he still couldn't figure out why. It became quite loud for a few seconds but then faded away and that was it for the whole forty five minutes.

As the time crawled by Martin couldn't help thinking about the next session with Madison and Jonathan. For some reason he had a feeling that it wouldn't be as much of an anti-climax as Josh's was proving to be. In the displays the column was still cold and hard-edged and waiting.

At exactly forty five minutes he turned on the lights to reveal a very relieved and smiling Josh.

'It wasn't that bad now, was it?' Martin said. 'Go on get writing then.'

Josh did just that. Martin turned to Jerzy.

'A bit boring that one, wasn't it?' Jerzy said in a low voice.

'Yes but I've got a feeling that the next one might be something special.'

'Why's that?'

'If I'm honest I'm not sure. Things happen when Madison's around but I had the distinct feeling that she was trying to control things in her last session, even then she wasn't all that successful. However, in his session, Jonathan had no control over whatever was happening with him. I just think that a few sparks might fly between them that's all.'

'Let's hope you're right,' Jerzy said as he stood up and stretched. 'It's pizzas after the next one, isn't it?'

'Yes, hungry already?'

'Well a bit. I'll definitely be ready for something soon.'

Martin looked around and noticed that Josh had stopped writing. Then again he supposed that he didn't have much to write about anyway. Josh followed him downstairs looking much happier than he had on the way up. Again three faces looked up at them but seeing the little smile on Josh's face they quickly looked away again.

Josh started writing up his second set of notes as Martin turned to Lydia.

'Just in case he's early can you keep an ear open for the pizza delivery man?' he asked.

'Yes of course,' Lydia replied.

As he handed her some cash Martin was aware that she was just about becoming his other assistant. He looked over at Madison and Jonathan who were up next. They glanced up apprehensively at Martin. He could see that they weren't looking forward to it.

Chapter Fifteen – Session 8: Jonathan and Madison

'Okay then, Madison, Jonathan, are you both ready?' Martin asked.

They gave each other a little sideways glance. Martin noticed Jonathan colouring a little as he caught Madison's eye.

'Well it's the last one for us, isn't it?' Madison said as she stood up.

'Yes that's right, the last one. There'll be pizzas after that.'

The mention of food didn't seem to cheer them up at all. Again they walked ahead of Martin up the stairs as if they were going to the executioner's block. Martin started to feel a bit guilty as he was actually looking forward to this session and the hoped for fireworks. They both sat down without a word and waited.

'God they're a really noisy pair, aren't they?' Jerzy whispered.

'I think they're both a bit scared and I've got a feeling that they have every right to be,' Martin said. He thought for a moment and then said, 'Oh it's no good I'll just have to be straight with them.'

Martin knew he'd only feel guilty afterwards so he went over and spoke to them.

'Look, I've got a feeling that this session might be at least as eventful as the previous ones you've been involved in.' He stopped and corrected himself. 'No, if I'm honest, I've got a feeling it might be a lot more eventful than the previous ones and I want to give you both one last chance. The door's just there and you can go through it right now and either go back to the hotel or hang around for pizzas. No-one will blame you if you do just that.' Madison was about to say something but Martin continued, 'You don't have to answer straight away. I want you to take a minute and think it over carefully.'

He went back and sat by Jerzy.

'Well that was very ethical of you,' Jerzy said with a smile.

'Oh well you know what they say, a puppy is for Christmas but guilt is for life. If anything does happen I want to make sure that I gave them every chance.'

After a minute had passed Martin went back to them.

'I'm ready,' Madison said with determination.

Jonathan hesitated for a moment before glancing over at Madison.

'Yes me too,' he eventually said.

'Thank you both,' Martin said and he meant it. 'Okay torches on and pads ready.'

He went over and turned off the lights.

Right from the start Martin had the prickly feeling that something was about to happen. The temperature of the column started pulsating and shadows started appearing against the blue coldness of the column in the thermal imaging camera. The low light camera showed nothing but blackness. Martin stared hard at the shadows but couldn't make anything of them. Now and again a shape or a face would appear and then quickly disappear. However he reckoned that this was just his brain trying to make some sense out of the randomness.

Martin was still sure that something was about to happen but nothing did. Each second crawled by as the tension was ratchetted up a little more. It was becoming unbearable. It didn't start until eighteen very slow minutes had passed. By the time he heard the sound of footsteps in the darkness he had started to feel slightly nauseous. These footsteps were different to the ones they'd heard before though. These were just footsteps, the sound of shoe leather on a hard surface.

The footsteps seemed far away at first but then they came closer.

'Where are you?' a man's voice said in a low menacing growl.

Martin knew that there was death and madness in that voice. How he knew that he didn't know, he just knew. The footsteps receded and there was silence. The silence stretched on and on as if it were an elastic band being pulled ever tighter. Then the elastic snapped.

'Where are you?' the voice demanded again with more urgency.

Again the silence but this time it only lasted a few seconds. It was shattered by the sound of a glass breaking as if dropped on the floor by accident. It was no accident as several more glasses followed in rapid succession. A shiver of fear went up Martin's spine and the rhyme started again in his head.

Janey and Johnny, sitting in a tree, K-I-S-S-I-N-G...

'Where are you bitch?' the voice was tight with emotion and shriller now.

A short silence was followed by the sharp deafening sounds of plates hitting the floor, not one by one but stacks of them at a time, and after that the hollower sound of cups being smashed. It seemed to go on forever. Then the footsteps began again, footsteps walking on broken glass.

Behind the rhyme another voice in his head was chanting...

'Safe, safe in the dark, keep small, don't breathe. Safe, safe in the dark...'

The footsteps and the voices faded away.

Jerzy wrote a note. It just had one word.

'WOW!'

Martin couldn't have agreed more. He looked over at the column. It was still sharp edged and very cold. The timer told him that the sounds had only lasted three and a half minutes. There was still a long way to go.

The taut silence lasted for a few minutes more before the two tone sound could be seen on the display. After what had just happened it somehow seemed like a friendly sound to Martin. He listened closely but it only just made it into his hearing range before it disappeared and once again there was silence.

The silence stretched on with the tension once again increasing with every second that passed. It was getting to Martin now and he wished that something would happen. It finally did.

'BOY!'

Martin jumped in his seat as the silence was broken by a man's voice gruffly shouting.

It was different to the first voice, an older man perhaps Martin thought.

'Boy! Where are you?'

Martin could sense the growing anger in the voice. He could also smell something and it wasn't nice. As the smell grew stronger he identified it as the smell of whisky and bad breath. It didn't help his nausea any.

'Boy, come here! You don't want to make Mr. Sausage angry now do you? You know what he's like when he's angry.'

Again he heard thoughts in his mind.

'Safe, safe in the dark, keep small, don't breathe. Safe, safe in the dark. Pray to God, pray to God. Safe, safe in the dark...'

The thoughts were becoming more desperate as the voice came nearer.

'Pray to God, pray to God. Safe, safe in the dark, safe...'

Then the deafening sound of plates hitting the floor and the hollower sound of cups being smashed. Then footsteps walking on broken glass.

'Where are you bitch?'

The smell of whisky and bad breath.

'BOY!'

Janey and Johnny, sitting in a tree, K-I-S-S-I-N-G...

Glass breaking, voices, smells all started to overlap each other and became a sort of mad symphony in Martin's head.

'Pray to God, pray to God. Safe, safe in the dark...'

He felt sick and he knew that he had to throw up. He wobbled towards the light switch and turned it on before heading straight out of the door into where the toilets used to be. There were cubicles but no toilets so he just threw up on the floor. He spat the last of it out and, feeling marginally better, made his way back. He stopped still as soon as he entered the door.

The lights were on but the sounds and the smells and the whole mad cacophony was still going on!

He looked over at the table and Jerzy was still there, soldiering on but his face was paler than he'd ever seen it before. Behind their table Madison and Jonathan were standing up. They were staring at the cold spot with glazed expressions as though they were hypnotised. They were also holding hands. Martin was starting to feel ill again.

'Madison, Jonathan!' Martin shouted.

They didn't seem to hear him.

Janey and Johnny, safe, safe in the dark, K-I-S, sitting in a tree, pray to God, S-I-N-G, God, safe, then comes marriage...

Martin's head felt like it was going to explode.

'MADISON, JONATHAN!' he shouted as loud as he could.

They turned their heads towards him and it was as though they didn't recognise him at first. Then the glazed expression left their faces and the sounds, smells and mental cacophony abruptly stopped. They looked at each other and then down at their hands. They quickly let go of each other's hand and sat down.

Martin's nausea also receded. He made it over to his two students.

'Are you okay?' he asked.

'Yes, we're fine,' they said.

It wasn't just the use of the word 'we' that Martin found strange. What really made him think was the fact that they'd said the words together. Not just together but precisely together. So together that they sounded like one voice.

However Martin had to admit that they both looked in better shape than either he or Jerzy did.

He sat down and looked at the displays. The column was still there but it had gotten considerably warmer. Martin wasn't at all surprised. He looked over at Madison and Jonathan who were both scribbling away at their notepads. He wondered how they'd managed to weather the quite considerable storm so well. He could only guess that, while the manifestations had come from them, for some reason they had been far less affected by them. He found that interesting.

He sat down beside Jerzy.

'Okay?' Martin asked.

'Better than I was,' Jerzy replied. 'I really thought I was going to throw up for a second there.'

He started backing up the data straight away.

Martin sat back and tried to think. He'd thought that the session might be intense but that was far worse than he could have ever imagined. He remembered one time when he'd been a kid and he'd gone to the funfair with his friends. He'd filled up with hot dogs and the fizziest possible drinks before getting on a waltzer. The violent spinning of the ride together with the overly loud music had produced results that were incredibly similar.

His peripheral vision caught a movement. He turned around. Jonathan and Madison were both standing up.

'We're finished,' they said together in precise unison.

Jonathan brought their notes over to Martin.

'Would it be okay with you if we went straight back to the hotel?' Jonathan asked. 'Madison isn't feeling too well,'

'Yes, yes of course,' Martin answered.

He was puzzled as to how Jonathan might know this as he and Madison hadn't said a word to each other since the session had ended. He looked over at Madison for confirmation. She nodded and Martin had to admit that she was looking quite pale.

'Jerzy will give you your phones back before you go and you've got my number. Please call me if you need anything or even if you just want to talk,' Martin said.

They both nodded at him. Jonathan's hand went out and Madison's hand grasped it with hers. They'd done this without looking at each other.

Martin wondered at this. It was the type of instinctive reaction that he'd only seen with couples that had been together for many years.

Martin and Jerzy accompanied them down. Lydia and Josh looked up at them. He saw that Lydia had noticed that Madison and Jonathan were holding hands and he also saw that she was puzzled by this.

Jerzy rescued their phones, gave Lydia a quick smile and a nod, and then returned upstairs. Without a word she followed him up. Martin opened the door for Madison and Jonathan and let them out, reminding them to call him if they needed anything.

He locked the door after they had left and leant against it. The session had been dark, intense and very strange, stranger that he could ever have imagined. Yet he found that Madison's and Jonathan's reactions after the event were much stranger still. He couldn't wait to find out why.

Chapter Sixteen – Jonathan and Madison

They walked back to the hotel down streets that were far from dark or empty. There was a still a fair amount of traffic on the roads, some shops open and there were even a few people walking around. They both walked as quickly as they could. Jonathan could feel Madison's need. Once in the hotel Jonathan followed Madison to her room.

No words were said and none were needed. They knew how each other felt and it was as natural to them as breathing.

Once inside she quickly stripped down to her bra and panties and got into bed. He left his T shirt and shorts on and climbed in after her. She had gotten into the middle of the bed and pulled herself into a tight foetal ball. He could feel her fear, her need to be in the dark, to make herself small and disappear. He'd known something like it himself. However thinking about her fear had somehow saved him from his own.

He got into bed and pulled her close into his body, wrapping his arms around her.

Janey and Johnny, sitting in a tree, K-I-S-S-I-N-G...

He could hear her rhyme in his head. He knew it had kept her safe.

He didn't say any words, he didn't need to. He soothed her as he told her with his feelings that she was safe and protected and that no harm could come to her. He would look after her. He could feel the dark fear in her heart receding as he made his feelings known to her. The tight ball of her body relaxed and she fell into a light sleep. While she slept he made sure that no fearful dreams came to her.

She only slept for a while as something woke her up. Nonetheless she felt refreshed. It was as if she'd slept for a week rather than just for an hour or so. She thought for a moment and realised what it was that had woken her up.

It was his need.

She could feel him, he needed to be touched, needed to be inside her. Along with that need there was fear, a fear of intimacy, a fear of failing, a fear of looking a fool. She turned and looked at his face. She realised that she knew everything about the man who now lay beside her.

Everything.

She also knew that he knew everything about her. Every one night stand, every bad, stupid and awful thing that she'd done was in his head. He knew it all and yet he still felt something for her. He still wanted her.

He'd never had sex before although how she knew this she didn't know. She knew and that was enough. She smiled and thought calming thoughts at him.

'Leave this to me,' she said as she pushed him onto his back.

His need and wanting for her had made her want him every bit as much. There was no need for foreplay. She undressed him, straddled him and put him inside her. She moved her hips and the pleasure was incredible. It took her a while for her to realise that she was not only feeling her pleasure but his too. They moved in perfect synchronicity as each knew exactly what the other needed. He nearly came and she could feel it. She slowed down and then built it up again, making the pleasure last as long as possible.

She could feel the pressure build up in him as he got closer to coming. At the same time the tentacles of an orgasm made itself known to her. When he came so did her orgasm. She could feel both at the same time and she felt as if she would explode with the intense pleasure she was experiencing. She knew that he felt it all too.

She rolled off him and they both lay there panting. Eventually they turned on their sides so they could look into each other's eyes.

'Is it always like that?' he asked in wonder.

'No, it's never like that. Never.'

Chapter Seventeen – Pizzas

Martin checked his watch, the pizzas were late. Josh had stopped scribbling in his notepad and was sitting quietly. He sat there thinking, still trying to process what had just happened. There seemed to be two distinct threads to the manifestations. The footsteps on broken glass he'd heard when Madison had been alone in the room and the 'Boy!' voice when Jonathan had been there. He'd felt the need to hide with both manifestations, to find a dark space and make himself small. The rhymes he'd heard in his head backed this up. They were a device that young children often use as a sort of magic to keep them safe when they're afraid.

He probably wouldn't be able to interview either of them for some days which he felt was a shame as he was itching to find out what was behind it all. He guessed that it was some sort of childhood trauma but what exactly? With regards to Jonathan at least he had a clue. The reference to 'Mr. Sausage' might indicate sexual abuse but what was behind Madison's dark visions? He knew that there was violence there. He could feel it in the words.

His thoughts were interrupted by the sound of knocking at the door. Food at last! He may have thrown up not long ago but now he suddenly felt ravenous.

'Can you give me hand?' Martin asked Josh.

It was the same delivery man. Rather than allow him in to wander around Martin held the door only half open so as to block his entry. He passed the pizzas and drinks to Josh to ferry to the table. Once all the food was in he paid the man and locked the door. He then went halfway up the stairs and shouted 'Pizzas' as loud as he could. Jerzy and Lydia came down a few seconds later and joined them.

Everyone seemed as hungry as Martin did and, although there should have been more than enough as Madison and Jonathan weren't there, Martin and Jerzy still found each other staring each other down for the last slice of peperoni.

Martin was just about to suggest a game of Rock, Paper, Scissors when Lydia swooped and grabbed it. This caused them all to burst out laughing. Martin thought it wasn't quite fair as she shared it with Jerzy anyway.

Even though Josh still had a session to go and Lydia had two, they were obviously feeling relieved that they were finally nearing the end. Martin couldn't blame them. He was feeling somewhat relieved himself. He didn't expect either of the last two sessions to be anywhere near as eventful as the last one had been.

No there's three sessions to go, he thought. He was nearly forgetting about the control session.

'What happened up there?' Josh asked. 'With Madison and Jonathan, am I allowed to ask?'

Martin gave this a little thought before answering.

'I'm sorry I can't go into details but I can say that a lot happened up there, perhaps too much. When I first set this up I'd have been happy with a fraction of what we've experienced here since we started. However, right this minute, I think I'd settle for a nice boring few hours to round it all off.'

'Yes me too,' Josh replied with sincerity.

Martin looked at his watch. It was nearly ten to two.

'Ready for the next one?' he asked as he stood up.

'Oh sure,' Lydia replied brightly.

Josh nodded and stood up. He had his notebook and torch and looked more than ready to get his last session over and done with.

Martin nodded and started for the stairs.

Chapter Eighteen – Session 9: Josh and Lydia

The first thing that Martin looked for once he turned out the lights was the display coming from the thermal imaging camera. The cold spot was still there and as sharply defined as ever. There was nothing showing on the other displays.

'It's gotten colder again,' Martin wrote.

'Not as cold as it was though,' Jerzy wrote back.

They sat in silence. Flat, blank, dark silence.

There was no prickling of the hairs on the back of his neck, no feeling of something about to happen, nothing. The room was just a room. He supposed that it would please Josh if his last session was entirely uneventful. After everything that had happened he wasn't sure if he'd be all that disappointed himself.

As the seconds dragged by Martin found himself thinking once again about the previous session. He started hypothesising about what might have triggered the manifestations when he heard a familiar voice in his head.

'Making bricks without straw again?'

This wasn't a manifestation but a memory. It was what his father always said when Martin went off on one of his flights of fancy. Martin smiled. He was right too. Hypothesising without hard facts is always bad practice.

He thought of his parents. They were getting on now and he realised with something of a shock that he hadn't seen them for a couple of weeks as he'd been too busy preparing for the experiment. He'd make time for a visit as soon as they were finished here, he told himself. He could do with a little break anyway before tackling the stacks of notes that he'd have to try and decipher.

He looked over at the clock. Only eight minutes had gone by. He had a feeling that this was going to be a long one. He thought again of his parents and smiled. He knew that without their support he would never have made it to university never mind to a professorship. He still had quite a way to go to beat his dad though. While he was Professor Jorgensen his father was definitely *the* Professor Jorgensen. Every time he met a fellow psychologist for the first time he was always asked if he was any relation to the famous Professor Anders Jorgensen.

He knew he had a mountain to climb to get anywhere near his father's achievements but he didn't mind that. Neither he nor his father felt as if they were in a competition though, his father always said that it was contributing that mattered most. If it was a large contribution or small one it didn't matter as we all stand on each other's shoulders.

In some ways he thought that he'd probably learnt more about life from his mum though. He remembered when he was struggling and feeling like he was getting nowhere his mother would always say 'Now stop and have a think. What was positive about today? What have you learnt that you didn't know when you woke up this morning?'

This usually worked and it was something he still asked himself whenever he felt frustrated or a bit down about how things were going. Lately his main frustrations had been with the university. He hadn't told Jerzy yet but he'd been trying to get him an Assistant Professor's job so that he'd get a proper wage for all the work he was putting in. He had to admit that it was largely selfish anyway, if Jerzy ever went he would leave a hole that would be impossible to fill.

So what had he learnt that he didn't know this morning? he asked himself.

There are ghosts. However they aren't 'out there' but inside us, the ghosts within, and they can manifest themselves as sounds and visions that can be recorded given the right circumstances. The circumstances being the right person in a low energy setting plus the thing that Jerzy called the 'ghost field'. That seemed to be the crucial factor in turning what was inside the dark recesses of our minds into palpable manifestations.

Into ghosts.

He corrected himself, it should have been the right people. Madison and Jonathan could both generate manifestations when they were on their own but together they were something else. Again Martin wondered if this might be behind what we called mediums. Perhaps there are people who can 'tune in' in some way to the ghost field. He also remembered Madison and Jonathan holding hands and his mind flashed up a picture of an old fashioned séance with everyone seated and holding hands.

He knew that what they'd found was important and that he'd possibly just started on a problem that might take him the rest of his life to solve, if he ever did. It felt right to him though, it felt like it was what he should be doing.

His ruminations were disturbed by the two tone sound. It seemed to be very far away and as fuzzy as ever. He looked over at the sound display. It got momentarily louder before disappearing and Martin had a tantalising 'tip of the tongue' moment when he almost remembered what it was that seemed so familiar. Then it was gone.

At exactly forty five minutes Martin turned on the lights.

'There that wasn't so bad,' Martin said as he turned towards Josh.

He was surprised to see Josh on his feet and looking quite pale. He was pointing towards the cold spot. Jerzy and Lydia stood up too when they saw it.

'How the fuck did that happen?' his assistant exclaimed.

Martin looked down the room. All of the phones on stands that had been placed at what seemed like random locations around the cold spot were now neatly arranged in a tight circle around the column.

'I take it that this is all on camera?' Martin asked.

Jerzy nodded.

'Didn't you pick up anything when the stands were being moved?' Martin asked.

Jerzy was tapping furiously away at his keyboard.

'I'm trying to pinpoint exactly when they were moved. I know I was half asleep after all that pizza but you'd have thought that the motion sensors would have alerted us if they were being moved but they didn't. Just give me a minute.'

Martin went over and had a close look. The makeshift stands were tightly packed around the cold spot forming a circle of around ten feet across. So they were now about three feet from the column of cold air. All of the wires still seemed to be connected. Martin thought he'd better ask anyway.

'Jerzy are you still getting readings? Are all the wires still connected?'

'Yes but the only problem is that the readings are saying that they're still in their original positions. We can see that they've all been moved but it hasn't registered on the displays yet. Do you want me to move them all back?'

Martin gave this some thought.

'No leave them where they are. There might be some reason for them being moved and, if there is, I want to find out what it is.'

'Er...I'm finished,' Josh interrupted with more than a little hesitation.

'Oh sorry Josh, Lydia, I was nearly forgetting about you,' he said as he accepted the notes from Josh. Lydia then gave him hers too. She was quiet and kept glancing towards the phone stands as though they might start moving again at any second.

'What do you want to do now?' Martin asked Josh.

'If it's okay I think I'd just as soon call it a day….well a night I suppose,' Josh said. 'Is there any point in doing the second set of notes? After all there's not much in those I just gave you.'

'No I suppose not. Fancy a coffee before you go?' Martin asked.

'Yeah sure,' Josh replied.

'How about you Jerzy?'

'Yes just give me a minute and I'll come down,' he said without raising his head.

Martin smiled at seeing Jerzy so nonplussed. It wasn't an expression that he'd seen on his assistant's face very often before. Then he looked at the tight circle of phone stands and his smile disappeared. Before this the manifestations had been mostly sounds with some visual components. Now 'it', whatever 'it' was, was not only messing with their minds but moving physical objects around as well.

Martin didn't know whether he should be worried by this or not. At that moment he was brutally aware of how little he actually knew about what was really happening in this room. Looking at the phone stands he felt real fear and this time it wasn't part of a manifestation.

Chapter Nineteen – Session 10: Lydia

As Lydia made the coffees Martin couldn't help but ask, 'Are you sure that you'll be okay for the next session?'

'Yes I'll be okay,' she replied reassuringly. 'I mean it just moved a few things around, nothing really frightening happened did it?'

A part of Martin agreed with her but another part was making warning noises in his head. If 'it' could move phone stands around then what else could it do?

A thought occurred to Martin. It was unlikely but it was worth pursuing.

'Did either of you think about the phone stands at all during the last session?' he asked as Lydia passed him a coffee.

He was desperately trying to find some rationale for what had happened. They both shook their heads.

He saw a smile appear on Lydia's face and he knew without looking around that Jerzy was coming down the stairs. When he joined them Martin asked him the same question.

'The phones?' Jerzy's face scrunched up with the effort of thinking. 'Oh yes I remember being quite bored and thinking something about possible layouts and what I could do with some newer phones. That was it really.'

It didn't really answer as to why the stands ended up in a perfect circle around the cold spot but it did remind Martin of something. It reminded him that he and Jerzy were part of the experiment too and he shouldn't ever forget that fact. As he thought this the two tone sound came back into his mind. It was the only manifestation that had been recorded at every session. If the sounds and visions could be traced back to real experiences then that would mean that it must have something to do with either him or Jerzy.

He knew it was most probably him. He'd heard that exact sound somewhere before but the memory remained tantalisingly out of reach.

'Anyway the strange thing is,' Jerzy continued, 'that the readings on the phones have snapped back and are now showing their real location, all grouped around the cold spot. It happened just before I came down.'

'Now that's strange. Some sort of time lag in the equipment perhaps?' Martin asked.

Jerzy shrugged.

'Could be but I'll know more when I do the full analysis.'

He noticed that Josh had finished his coffee and was packing his notebook into his backpack. He stood up and held his hand out towards Martin.

'See you then Professor, I'm going to go and get some sleep. It's been...well...it's been different,' Josh said managing a smile.

Martin shook his hand.

'Thanks Josh and yes I have to agree that it's been very different. Here I'll let you out.'

Josh waved goodbye to Jerzy and Lydia.

'I'll probably see you next week some time, you know for the follow up interview,' Martin said as he held the door open.

'I'll look forward to it,' Josh said.

As Martin locked the door again he couldn't help thinking how Josh had looked as he stepped out into the street. He turned around to face Jerzy and Lydia.

'He looked so relieved that it was over for him. I never thought I'd say it but I must admit that I'll be glad when it's all over too,' he said.

'Well just the two sessions to go now prof,' Jerzy said trying to be positive.

'Yes just the two,' he echoed. 'Are you ready then Lydia?'

She nodded and picked up her notebook and torch.

Just the two left, he said to himself.

Again the room felt flat as they waited in the dark for something to happen. The displays were all static and the column temperature was too. It was very cold but Martin didn't feel any 'energy' in the room, the hairs standing up on the back of his neck and the feeling that something was about to happen. He wasn't sorry either. They'd gotten more than enough from the other sessions, enough data to keep him and Jerzy happy for months.

Jerzy was writing something.

'Mr. Two Tone again.'

It was so low that Martin could only just about hear it but the sound display showed it clearly enough. Jerzy was writing again.

'It's going around the cold spot, circular path.'

Martin strained to try and pick up what the sound was trying to say to him. It sounded like a question but what was it?

The peaks diminished and the sound disappeared. He looked at the clock. Twenty two minutes gone.

Nearly halfway there, he told himself.

He was beginning to feel something. A strange sort of anxiety was building in him. It wasn't like anything he'd felt before and it definitely felt like it was coming from within him and not from the outside. He could see shapes and shadows in the cold spot, flickering shapes, shapes that looked like tongues of fire. He looked more closely. He saw red and yellow flames, he could feel the heat on his skin, hear the loud crackling sound as they devoured everything. His left arm started hurting.

The two tone sound came back. It was louder than ever. Martin's anxiety grew and despite the cold he found that he was sweating now. What was happening to him? He had no idea and no control over it whatsoever.

The sound became louder still. A question was being asked but what was it? Then it became all too clear.

Martin remembered when he'd been a child and his father was showing him how an old analogue radio worked. At first all he'd heard was crackles and ghostly voices until his father got it tuned in just right and then suddenly a voice clearly rang out from across the miles. A man with an American accent spoke as if he'd been in the same room. Now another voice spoke and it was in the same room.

It was a little boy's voice. It was plaintive and sad and he sounded lost.

'Martwen? Martwen, where are you?' the little voice asked.

The fireflies were streaming from the column and rotating around the cold spot at a dizzying speed. They were red and yellow, the colour of fire, the colour of flames.

'Martwen? Martwen, where are you?' the little voice asked again.

Martwen? There was something at the back of Martin's mind that he'd always thought had been a wall. This was where his mind and his memories ended, or so he'd thought. He could feel the wall crumbling to dust.

'Martwen?' the voice pleaded again.

Behind the wall there was a door. It swung open.

The memories of a former life came swooping out at him like clouds of black bats flying out of a cave. Every memory stung.

In the pain he remembered.

'Eddie? Eddie is that you?' Martin asked as he stood up. 'Is that really you?'

'Martwen? I can't hear you Martwen,' the little voice sounded afraid.

Martin started walking towards the cold spot. As he did so the fireflies came together and coalesced into a bright shining figure. Martin could see it clearly. It was a little boy aged just over three years old. He had a dirty old T shirt on that served as his pyjamas and his sock bear was dangling from his hand. The tears ran like rivers down Martin's face as he recognised him.

'Eddie, I'm here Eddie. Can't you see me?'

'Martwen, is that you? It's dark here, it's dark here Martwen.'

Visions came into Martin's head, visions of fire and flames, of things burning. He coughed as he inhaled the acrid smell of smoke. He could feel the skin on his left arm starting to blister and the pain was intense. He heard someone shouting from behind him but it meant nothing to him. The anxiety in his chest became unbearable, tighter and tighter. He could smell the smoke, he could feel the heat on his skin and he could hear Eddie's screams. His left arm was now on fire and the pain was excruciating.

'Martwen! Martwen!'

He felt a weight of sadness descend on him that was utterly unbearable. Raw despair and hopelessness rolled over him like a tidal wave. He couldn't fight it and it broke his heart.

Then it all went black.

Jerzy had been shouting at Martin to come back. He could hear the sounds, the little voice pleading in his headphones. He also picked up the sound of Martin as he hit the floor. As he struggled to get his headphones off he heard the little voice start to say something but Jerzy didn't hang around the find out what it was. He ran into the darkness to where he thought the light switch should be but it took him a few seconds to locate it and he started to panic.

Then he found it and the lights came on.

Martin was lying on his side a few feet away from where the phone stands were grouped around the cold spot. Jerzy ran over to him closely followed by Lydia. He could see that Martin was breathing but he couldn't think what to do next. Lydia felt for his pulse and shot Jerzy a concerned look.

'His heart's racing,' she said. 'It's beating far too fast, call for an ambulance. He needs help. Now Jerzy!'

Jerzy didn't need to be asked twice. He raced down the stairs, found his phone and dialled 999 straight away. The operator had to calm him down before she got all the information she needed. She told him that a paramedic was on his way and it would help if he waited outside so they could be sure that they'd gotten the right address.

Jerzy waited anxiously outside and started pacing up and down the street. What the hell had just happened? It had been so quick that it was all just a jumble in his mind.

He heard the siren and waved down the paramedic's car when it came around the corner. He led the paramedic upstairs. Lydia had managed to get Martin into the recovery position and she had her hand on his wrist.

'His pulse is very fast,' she said to the paramedic.

He felt the pulse too.

'I'll just be a minute,' he said before he raced back down the stairs.

He came back and pulled a hypodermic out of a sterile package and jabbed it into Martin. He waited for a few seconds and then felt his pulse again.

'It's slowing a little,' he said with a reassuring smile.

He got his radio out and requested an ambulance immediately. They heard him say the words 'severe tachycardia'. Jerzy and Lydia looked at each other. It sounded serious.

'Can you do me a favour? Will one of you wait outside for the ambulance and show them up here as soon as they arrive?'

Jerzy nodded and made for the door. He looked back before he left the room and managed to give Lydia a half a smile. He was so glad that she was there.

A couple of minutes later the ambulance arrived and two ambulance men got out. He told them about the stairs. They took a stretcher out and wheeled it towards the door. They pulled the wheels up when they came to the stairs and carried it up. Once upstairs they positioned the stretcher on the floor next to Martin and had a quick discussion with the paramedic. Between them they managed to manoeuvre Martin onto the stretcher and then strapped him securely in. The paramedic came over to Jerzy.

'It would be quicker if we could carry him down the stairs as he is. Would you be okay to take a handle?'

Jerzy nodded.

The four of them took a handle each and managed to get the stretcher down the stairs with little bother. Once at the bottom the ambulance men dropped the wheels and made for the door. Jerzy and Lydia followed them.

'Is it okay if we come?' Lydia asked. 'In the ambulance I mean.'

'Of course,' one of the ambulance men replied. 'Once we've got your friend inside just jump in.'

Jerzy turned off the power and locked the steel door behind him before joining Lydia inside the ambulance.

He didn't remember much about the ride afterwards. He could hear the siren. It was like a reminder that this was all real, that this was serious. He felt scared, he didn't want to lose Martin. He was his best friend. It all started to get to him and he started shaking. He felt an arm around him and a hand holding his. He turned and looked at Lydia with complete and utter gratitude.

Once they arrived at the hospital Martin was whizzed into an emergency ward and Jerzy and Lydia were left in the hallway outside. A few minutes later the ambulance men came out wheeling an empty stretcher.

'Bye then,' they said.

Then one of them stopped and came back.

'You did okay back there, you did the right thing,' he said before he walked off.

Jerzy could only nod. He had no idea what to say. He turned to Lydia.

'You did the right thing is what he meant. Thanks I was…I just didn't know…'

She held his head in her hands and wiped a tear from his eye with her thumb.

'It's okay, it's always hard when it's someone you love. I know that all too well myself.'

She kissed him and it was truly the only thing in the world that could have made him feel any better.

He smiled at Lydia and then a look of shock appeared on his face.

'Liz, oh my God, I better call his wife Liz, hadn't I?'

He stood up and took a few deep breaths before he rang the number. He walked up and down as he tried to explain. It was a short conversation. It was the middle of the night and he'd woken Liz up but nevertheless she was in the car and on her way into London within a matter of minutes.

Waiting in the quiet and banal reality of a hospital corridor Jerzy wondered what in God's name had just happened.

And who on earth was Eddie?

Chapter Twenty – Straight afterwards

Liz ran down the hallway towards them. She looked as though she'd just thrown some clothes on at random which is exactly what she'd done.

'Where is he? What's happened? Is he alright?' she asked breathlessly.

'I don't know Liz, I just don't know,' Jerzy replied. 'They haven't told us anything yet.'

One look at his face made her think the worst.

Lydia spotted this.

'Liz, I'll go in and ask. I'll tell them that you're here,' she said.

Liz nodded her gratitude and sat down next to Jerzy.

'I'm sorry Liz,' Jerzy said. 'I'm so sorry.'

Liz squeezed his hand.

'It's not your fault Jerzy, I know that. I had a bad feeling about this one, I told him that he'd bite off more than he could chew but you know Martin, he wouldn't listen. He never bloody listens,' she said.

A white coated doctor came out and sat next to Liz.

'You're Mr. Jorgensen's wife?' she asked.

'Yes, I'm Elizabeth Jorgensen. How is he? Is he…' she couldn't finish the sentence.

'He's stable for the moment. Tell me has he ever had any heart problems before?'

'No, never.'

'Has he had any symptoms such as chest pain, light headedness, palpitations or fainting fits before?'

Liz shook her head.

'Any incidences of high blood pressure?'

'No, nothing like that. God he's only thirty nine, are you telling me that he's got a heart problem?'

The doctor looked puzzled.

'All I can say at the moment is that he's had a severe tachycardic episode, that's when the heart beats abnormally fast. It's usually an indication of a heart problem that's gone undiagnosed for some reason but we haven't found anything as yet that might explain it.'

'Will he be okay?' Liz asked gripping Jerzy's hand even more tightly.

'I'm afraid that it's too early to be sure. I'll come out and update you when we know something more.'

The doctor smiled and left them. They looked at each other with a lost and helpless expression. Liz sat down and looked down at her hands. Lydia sat by her and held her hand.

'I'm sorry,' Liz said, 'I never even asked you your name.'

'It's Lydia,' Jerzy said. 'She's one of Martin's students.' He looked at her and his heart suddenly filled up. 'She's my girlfriend,' he added.

Liz looked in Lydia in something like amazement.

'Yes, I'm his girlfriend,' Lydia confirmed giving Jerzy a smile.

'She was fantastic tonight, I don't know what I'd have done without her,' Jerzy said.

'Well Martin didn't say anything but I must admit that I'm glad. You've chosen well Jerzy,' Liz said as she gave Lydia's hand a squeeze.

The three of them waited and drank machine coffee and then waited some more. The sun had risen before the doctor returned.

'We think he's out of danger,' she said with a smile.

'Oh thank God, thank...' Liz managed to say before the tears came.

Lydia gave her a hug while shedding a few tears herself. Jerzy turned away as he wiped the tears from his face.

'We'll need to keep him in for some tests. There's something going on that we can't quite figure out as yet. He briefly woke up and became very agitated. He started crying and he said the name 'Eddie' over and over. Have you any idea who Eddie is?'

They all shook their heads. Jerzy briefly explained what they'd been doing just before Martin had collapsed.

'He said the name Eddie a few times before he collapsed but I've no idea who Eddie might be. He's never mentioned the name before.'

'Me neither,' Liz confirmed.

'Well we've had to sedate him I'm afraid so he'll be out for at least another four or five hours. You can go and sit with him if you'd like,' the doctor said.

Liz nodded her gratitude once more. They followed the doctor into a curtained off bay. Behind the curtain they saw Martin lying on a hospital bed. He was hooked up to a series of machines all of which seemed to be beeping away. He lay still and white faced, he had an oxygen mask on his face. Liz sat by him and took his hand in hers.

'Idiot!' she said with feeling before she bent over and gently kissed his cheek.

Jerzy felt better after seeing him.

'Is all your equipment still back at the pub?' Liz asked.

Jerzy nodded.

'You might as well go and pack it all up and come back in a while,' Liz said.

'Are you sure?' Jerzy asked.

In truth he'd forgotten all about his gear and he realised that he couldn't leave it there for much longer. He wasn't even sure if the last session had been backed up properly.

'Go on, go. I'll be okay and he isn't going anywhere,' Liz said as she nodded at Martin.

They phoned for a taxi and both of them sat in the back when it came. As the taxi drove off Lydia grasped Jerzy's hand.

'Did you really mean what you said back there?' she asked. 'About me being your girlfriend?'

'Yes I did. After I said it I was a bit scared if I'm honest. It was okay to say that, wasn't it?' he said nervously.

'You didn't say it just because you were grateful or anything like that?' she asked.

'I'm grateful of course, you were so good tonight, but no it's more than that. I like you, I mean I really like you.'

She pulled his head down and gave him a long, intense kiss.

'Good, so it's official now,' she said with smile.

As soon as Jerzy got back to the pub he checked that everything had been recorded and then backed it all up. With Lydia helping it didn't take him long to pack everything away. He was about to unplug the thermal imaging camera when he noticed something strange.

'Here look at this,' he said to Lydia.

Lydia looked at the small screen.

'There's nothing there,' she said with a puzzled face.

'That's right, there's nothing there,' Jerzy replied.

He walked down towards the bottom of the room, to where the phone stands were still tightly grouped in a circle. He moved some of them out of the way and held his hand out. He then moved it around.

'The cold spot,' Jerzy said. 'It's gone!'

Chapter Twenty One – A bit later

Liz was still sitting beside Martin when they got back. She had her eyes closed but she opened them and sat up when they came towards Martin's bed.

'I'm sorry, I must have drifted off there for a moment,' she said as she rubbed her eyes.

Jerzy listened out for the heart monitor. The beeping was reassuringly slow.

'How's he doing?' he asked.

'They think he'll be okay but there's a remote chance of blood clots or a stroke so they're going to keep him in for at least a week.'

'A stroke?' Jerzy said looking concerned.

'A remote chance they said. From what they told me this tachycardia's got them really puzzled. They've no idea what caused it yet so they've no idea what the risk factors might be,' Liz said. 'Tell me Jerzy, what happened back there?'

Jerzy did his best to explain.

'We were doing the last session with Lydia and I honestly didn't think that anything was going to happen. We've had this strange two tone sound that been appearing in every session but we thought nothing of it. It was usually at a very low sound level and it just came and went. This time it stayed. It was muffled before so you couldn't make out what it was but this time it came in loud and clear.'

'What was it?' Liz asked.

'It was a child's voice, a little boy. He had a lisp. I think he was trying to say Martin's name but he pronounced it 'Martwen' instead.'

'Did you see anything?'

'Not clearly, I just saw a sort of bright light when all the fireflies, sorry they weren't real fireflies, they were like little dots of light. Anyway they all came together. I couldn't make out what it was but Martin knew. He said the name 'Eddie' several times,' Jerzy said.

'Eddie?' Liz said. 'I've never heard of an Eddie before.'

'Me neither. I suppose we'll just have to wait until he wakes up then,' Jerzy said.

'Perhaps his parents might know,' Liz said. 'Oh Christ his parents! What was I thinking of? I should have called them straight away.'

Jerzy and Lydia went down to get some breakfast in the hospital café while she did this. Liz didn't want to leave Martin so they promised to bring her something back. Despite everything Jerzy found he was hungry. He had no problem putting away a bacon sandwich while Lydia just settled for toast and coffee.

'What do you think happened?' Lydia asked.

Jerzy shrugged.

'I've no idea, the whole thing just feels like a bad dream right now, a really surreal one at that. Every time I think about it I have to ask myself if it really happened.'

'I know exactly what you mean. I remember catching the train down here but it seems like a lifetime ago now.'

'I'm glad you made it,' Jerzy said.

'Me too. What will you need to do next?' she asked.

'I'll need to analyse all the data and God knows there's more than enough of it.'

'Can I help?' she asked.

'That would be great, well better than great actually.'

As they walked into Martin's bay they could hear sounds. Martin was moving his head from side to side and making a sort of grunting sound.

'Can you tell the doctor that Martin's waking up? She said to tell her as soon as possible,' Liz asked.

Lydia went off and returned with the doctor a few seconds later. The doctor looked at the monitors. She went off and returned with a hypodermic needle in a plastic sterile pack.

'He was quite distressed the last time he was conscious. This is a sedative just in case,' the doctor explained.

Martin's eyelids started to flutter open.

'Mr. Jorgensen, can you hear me?' the doctor asked. 'I'm a doctor and you're in hospital.'

'Hospital?' Martin whispered. He looked around but it was clear that he wasn't seeing them but something else. 'Eddie, Eddie I can't see you. Eddie! Where are you?'

He started crying uncontrollably and the beeping of the heart monitor started to speed up.

'Eddie where are you?' he shouted again as his body jerked from side to side.

The beeping got faster still. The doctor quickly injected Martin with the syringe and the pace of the beeping slowed down again.

'We'll just have to try again later. I've given him a slightly stronger dose so it's going to be at least another eight hours before he wakes up again,' the doctor said.

'What is it? What's happening to him?' Liz said the fear evident in her voice.

'I'll be honest,' the doctor said, 'I've no idea. My best guess is that we're dealing with some sort of mental trauma and, if that is the case, then the sedative and sleep should help. We can only see what happens the next time he wakes up.'

'So it's just waiting then,' Liz said bleakly.

Jerzy sat down and suddenly felt exhausted.

'Have you two had any sleep?' Liz asked.

They both shook their heads.

'Go and get some sleep then. There's nothing you can do here. I'll need you when he wakes up,' Liz said.

Jerzy couldn't fault Liz's logic so he drove Lydia back to the hotel. He stopped outside Lydia's room, kissed her and said he'd knock on her door in six hours or so.

'You don't have to,' Lydia said. 'I've got an alarm clock in my room and we can both use that, if you want to that is.'

It took a moment for what she was proposing to register with Jerzy.

'You mean you want me to stay?' he asked. 'With you?

'I don't want to be alone right now,' she said.

She unlocked her door and held it open for him. They sat on the edge of the bed and Jerzy took her hand in his.

'Are you sure?' he asked feeling somewhat breathless.

'I am,' she replied.

'Me too.'

For some reason, as tired as they were, neither of them got much sleep.

Chapter Twenty Two – The True Story

They got back to the hospital around three in the afternoon. As they approached Martin's bed Jerzy put his finger to his lips. Liz was asleep in the chair. Martin was still out cold and the beeping of the heart monitor was slow and regular. Jerzy pointed towards the hallway and Lydia followed him outside.

'Might as well let her sleep until he wakes up,' Jerzy said.

'The doctor said he'd be out for eight hours so hopefully we should know something before long,' Lydia said.

They sat there in silence for a while. They held each other's hands and waited for something to happen.

About twenty minutes later a couple in their seventies came along the hallway towards them. They seemed to be somewhat agitated and confused.

'We've been walking around in circles. Oh what was the name of that ward again?' the man asked as he gave the woman an exasperated look.

The woman was about to reply when Jerzy stood up and interrupted her.

'Mr. and Mrs. Jorgensen! How are you? I don't know if you remember me but I'm...'

It was Jerzy's turn to be interrupted.

'Oh thank God!' the man said. 'Look Alice, it's Martin's friend Jerzy.'

'How is he Jerzy?' Mrs. Jorgensen asked as she gave him a worried look.

'He's okay I think, he's under sedation at the moment but he should be waking up in the next hour or so,' Jerzy replied.

'How's Liz? Is she in there?' Mr. Jorgensen asked as he nodded towards the ward door.

'Yes, she was asleep when we last looked. She's been awake most of the night.'

'Stay here Anders and I'll have a peek,' Mrs. Jorgensen ordered.

Mr. Jorgensen sat down next to Jerzy. He was tall and thin with grizzled grey hair and a grey beard. He had a rumpled old brown tweed suit on and a brown flat cap which he took off and twirled nervously in his hand. Jerzy had only met Professor Anders Jorgensen two or three times before and he was still somewhat in awe of him. 'Jorgensen's Theory of Personality' was in just about every textbook and it was one of the most cited psychological works of all time.

They sat and exchanged nervous smiles while they waited in suspense to hear how Martin was doing. A few minutes later Alice Jorgensen came out. She had long grey hair and was bundled up in a dark blue duffle coat. She had a natural air of authority about her that reminded Lydia of a teacher she'd once had, one she'd liked very much. She gave them all a strained smile.

'I had a quick word with the doctor. As you said Jerzy he's still under sedation and they won't know any more until he wakes up. Liz is still asleep too so it might be best if we just wait out here for a while,' she said as she sat down next to her husband.

She looked at Jerzy and then at Lydia. She did it once again but Jerzy still didn't get the hint.

'Aren't you going to introduce us?' she finally asked.

'Oh yes of course. I'm sorry this is Lydia, she's my girlfriend,' he replied as he flashed Lydia a smile. 'She was with us when it happened. She looked after Martin while I waited outside for the ambulance. She was great.'

'Thank you my dear,' Alice said as she reached over and touched Lydia's hand. 'Now Jerzy tell us exactly what happened.'

Jerzy briefly explained the history of the Black Vaults and the reason why Martin had set up the experiment. He told them of the extraordinary nature of the cold spot and some of the phenomena that they'd observed.

'And you have all this recorded and backed up?' Anders asked.

'Oh yes I made sure of that,' Jerzy replied.

'Fascinating,' Anders replied. 'You know I'd really like to...'

'Enough about the experiment,' Alice said giving her husband a stern look. 'What happened to Martin?'

'Well it was the last but one session and there was just Martin, myself and Lydia in the room. It hard to explain but it felt flat, every time before you could feel the energy building up before something happened. Anyway this sound that we'd heard at every session came back. I didn't think anything of it at the time. We'd never made out what it was and it had always faded away before. This time it suddenly became louder and crystal clear. I could hear that it was a child's voice and he was calling for someone, someone called Martwen.'

Jerzy noticed a look of shock on Alice's face as her hand went up and covered her mouth.

'Then there was some sort of visual phenomenon too but it just looked like a ball of light to me. However it obviously meant something to Martin. He stood up and then started walking towards it.'

'What did the voice say?' Anders asked.

'He was calling 'Martwen' over and over again. As Martin walked closer he asked 'Eddie is that you?' It was as if he saw something in the ball of light that I couldn't. Have you any idea who Eddie might be?' Jerzy asked.

Alice and Anders looked at each other. Jerzy thought that they looked a little scared.

'You've heard about this Eddie before haven't you?' Jerzy asked. 'You know who he is.'

Anders and Alice exchanged looks again.

'Yes I know who Eddie is and so does Martin, he's just forgotten that he knows that's all,' Anders said.

'Yet Liz said that's she had no idea who Eddie was,' Jerzy said.

'No he never told Liz, he never told anyone...'

'Never told me what Anders?' Liz said as she walked out of the ward towards them. 'What?'

Alice stood up and went over to Liz.

'Just give me a minute dear, please,' she pleaded and disappeared into the ward.

Alice appeared a few seconds later.

'There's a relatives room just down the hall. I think we might be able to talk better in there.'

Anders followed Alice inside but Jerzy and Lydia made no move to follow.

'Jerzy, Lydia you come too,' Liz said.

'But we're not family or anything,' Jerzy protested.

'I think you both deserve to hear whatever they've got to tell us,' Liz said.

Alice and Anders didn't look at all surprised when Jerzy and Lydia accompanied Liz in to the room where they all sat down except for Anders. Jerzy thought he looked like he was about to give a lecture or something.

'Liz, one of the reasons you called us was because you said that the doctors needed to know if there was any history of heart disease in the family or any sudden unexplained deaths. You hoped that we could confirm this one way or the other,' Anders said. 'I'm afraid that we can't give you that information.'

'Why?' Liz exclaimed. 'Why on earth wouldn't you want to tell the doctors something that might help your own son?'

Alice took Liz's hand in hers and squeezed it.

'Because Martin isn't our son,' Anders said.

'What?' Liz almost shouted. 'What do you mean he isn't your son?'

'I think I said that wrong,' Anders replied. 'He is our son and he always will be our son but what I meant is that we are not biologically related. We adopted Martin when he was five years old. We don't know anything about his family's medical history.'

It was obvious that Liz was struggling to process this new information.

'But why? Why didn't he tell me? Why didn't you tell me?' she said her voice rising.

'We talked about this many times, Alice and I, and we felt that it was up to Martin to tell you himself. If I'm honest we were never quite sure if Martin had genuinely forgotten about his previous life or if he just didn't want to talk about it. It might seem from what you've told us that he had genuinely forgotten.'

'Forgotten what?' Liz asked.

'Let me start at the beginning,' Anders said. 'As you know Liz we live just outside Cambridge and many years ago a colleague of mine, knowing my interest in young children and how personality developed, asked me if I'd be interested in seeing a patient of his, a young five year old boy called Martin Brownson who was in care. I was more than happy to get involved and even more so once I heard about the child's background. I found that I became interested in him, looking back I was probably too interested. It's not good for a psychologist to empathise too much with a patient but with Martin I just couldn't help myself. Anyway after what happened his mother was convicted of neglect and she was released from prison after serving seven months. I learnt that she died of an overdose within weeks of coming out and so Martin became an orphan. Then my colleague became ill and so I took over Martin's case. We became even closer, I even brought him home to see Alice a few times.'

'Brought him to see me indeed,' Alice interrupted. 'He let it drop one evening that Martin was being put up for adoption. Anders, like most psychologists, is smart and devious. He didn't say any more about it but the idea was planted in my head. A few days later I suggested that we should apply to adopt him ourselves and Anders seemed quite surprised. However, I later noticed that he had all the forms ready for signing and had already spoken to someone at the orphanage about it. Luckily they thought it would be a good idea too. And so Martin came to live with us.'

Alice gave Liz a huge smile.

'I can't explain what it was like. We had a nice life and a beautiful house and we could do whatever we liked. But when Martin came to stay everything changed. The only way I can explain it is that it was like we'd been living in black and white before and suddenly our world was now in technicolour. Martin had a habit of drawing on the walls when he was young and so our house wasn't quite as pristine as it was before but I didn't care. The house became something much better, it became a home. Every little thing we did became an adventure, even an afternoon trip to the local park was better than any holiday I'd ever had before that. He was a delight to be with, a very special child.'

Anders smiled at his wife and then the smile disappeared.

'He was a very troubled child when he first came to us though,' Anders said. 'After such a trauma it was only to be expected. He hardly said a word and he couldn't read or write at all. If I'm honest I don't think he'd ever seen a book until he went into care. Alice and I worked as hard with him as we could and he gradually improved. A year later you wouldn't have recognised him, he'd turned into a real chatterbox and he was doing very well in school.'

'What was the trauma?' Liz asked in a near whisper.

Anders and Alice exchanged concerned looks again.

'Martin's mother was a woman called Judy Brownson,' Anders explained. 'She was in her early thirties and she was a part-time barmaid, a part-time prostitute and a full-time drug addict. She lived in a sink estate in Cambridge in a squalid little house, when she was there that is. No-one knew about Martin, neither the social or educational systems had any idea that Martin existed. Martin or his brother.'

'He has a brother? Liz asked.

'No, not anymore,' Anders replied softly. 'Anyway Martin and his brother were used to being left alone and they survived somehow. Afterwards some of the neighbours came forward and told about how they'd seen Martin regularly raiding their waste bins looking for food. Why they never thought to report this at the time is still a mystery to me. Well one bitterly cold night they were in this shithole of a house alone,' Anders said, the anger clear in his voice. 'They had no electricity, no light, no heating, nothing. Martin said that at the time it happened his brother was ill, he was coughing and shaking a lot of the time. It was so cold in the house that he said ice had formed on the inside of the windows.'

'How do you know all this?' Liz asked.

'I got some of it from the people who investigated the case and from my colleague but most of it I got from Martin himself. He only told me fragments of the story at any one time but I was eventually able to piece it all together. Anyway Martin and his brother were very close, they only had each other after all, and so he tried to help him. He tried to start a fire to warm the living room up so his brother would stop shaking and get well again. Unfortunately one of the matches slipped out of his hand as he tried to light it, his little hand was probably frozen and he couldn't grip it properly. Anyway the match fell on some old newspapers that he was going to use as fuel for the fire and they caught light. There was so much crap in that house that the whole place went up like a bonfire.'

Anders looked over at Liz. A tear was falling down her cheek.

'He tried to get to his brother but he couldn't, the fire had taken hold too quickly. He said that he could hear his brother calling to him from the bedroom but the fire was between them. He had a bit of a speech impediment and he called him 'Martwen'. He was still calling when Martin ran out of the house. He blamed himself for leaving his brother but he couldn't have done any more. I found out that the clothes he'd been wearing had been actually charred by the heat of the fire and that he'd been quite badly burnt on one arm too.'

'Yes, his left arm,' Liz said. 'There are some marks there but he'd never say what caused it.'

'The fire brigade arrived a few minutes later and Martin was still standing on the street when they brought his brother's body out wrapped in a red blanket. His little feet were sticking out, one foot had a sock on and the other was bare. Martin remembered that.'

'Oh my God!' Liz exclaimed. 'Why didn't he tell me?'

'Guilt, he blamed himself for his brother's death. He took it all on himself. We did our best to explain that it wasn't his fault, none of it was, but I was never sure if he ever realised that emotionally,' Anders said.

'We even thought of telling you ourselves but there never seemed to be a good time,' Alice added.

'What was his name?' Liz asked.

'His brother?' Anders asked. 'It was Edward, Martin called him Eddie.'

Chapter Twenty Three – Martin wakes up

An ominous silence gripped the room after Anders had spoken. When the door opened most of them started with surprise. It was a nurse.

'Mrs. Jorgensen, your husband is starting to wake up,' he said. 'The doctor was wondering if you wanted to come.'

'Of course,' Liz said as she jumped up. She was half out of the door when she looked back. 'Alice, will you come with me?'

Alice smiled and left holding Liz's hand. Anders and Jerzy sat down.

'That was some story,' Jerzy said. 'I'd never have guessed.'

'Yes, we all have our secrets but while we have some time tell me all about the experiment,' Anders asked. 'I'd like to know how you set it up and what Martin was hoping to discover from it.'

This made Jerzy smile. While he was Martin's dad he was also a psychologist to his bones.

Alice sat on one side of Martin's bed while Liz sat on the other. He was moving his head from side to side and his eyelids would momentarily open and then close again. A few minutes later the doctor joined them.

'Mr. Jorgensen,' she said loudly, 'can you hear me? You're in the hospital.'

Liz saw Martin's lips make the shape of the word 'hospital'.

'You need to wake up now Mr. Jorgensen,' the doctor said again as Martin's eyelids started to droop.

'What?' he said and for the first time he opened his eyes properly.

Liz took his hand in hers and gave it a squeeze. He turned his head and looked at his wife.

'Liz? What happened?' he croaked.

'Would you like a drink Mr. Jorgensen?' the doctor asked.

Martin nodded. The doctor handed Liz a non-drip beaker of water. She held it to Martin's lips and he drank a few drops.

'Do you know why you're here?' the doctor asked.

They could see Martin thinking but his mind was a blank. He shook his head.

'Do you remember being in the pub, the...' the doctor stopped and looked questioningly at Liz.

'The Black Vaults,' Liz said.

'Yes, you were in the Black Vaults. It was a psychology experiment. Do you remember?'

Martin tried to think but his memories were vague and slippery. It took him some time before anything came back to him.

'I remember,' he said. 'It was cold and Jerzy was there.'

He thought some more and the memories suddenly flooded in. They overwhelmed him.

'Eddie! I saw Eddie,' he said and started crying again. 'Oh he sounded so lonely, so lonely and lost.'

The tears flowed and Liz held her husband's hand as he sobbed his heart out. He didn't stop crying even as the doctor took his temperature and blood pressure. She disappeared and came back a little later with some pills.

'Please take these Mr. Jorgensen. They'll help you to sleep,' the doctor said as she handed Liz two white pills.

'What are they?' Liz asked.

'They're a sort of sedative but nowhere near as strong as the one we gave him before. They'll help him sleep and that's what he needs right now, it will help him to process the trauma.'

Liz gave him the tablets and then took his hand in hers again. The tears gradually subsided and he eventually drifted off to sleep again.

'Come on Liz', Alice said. 'You need to look after yourself too. Have you had anything to eat?'

Liz shook her head.

'Jerzy brought me something earlier but I wasn't hungry.'

'Come on then, let's find the café and get you fed.'

Alice wasn't at all surprised when she opened the door of the relative's room to hear her husband quizzing Jerzy about the finer details of the equipment he'd used during the experiment. He stopped when she came in.

'How is he?' he asked.

'They've given him a lighter sedative and he's sleeping again. Anyway enough shop talk,' Alice said. 'Liz needs some food and I dare say you'll be hungry by now too Anders.'

'I'll show you where the café is,' Jerzy said.

Liz was surprised at how hungry she felt once she saw the food on display. They all ate in silence. After they'd finished Liz turned to Anders.

'You must have dealt with similar cases before, Anders. What do you think will happen to him?' she asked.

He looked at her and then became thoughtful.

'He's had quite a shock and, if it is just the mental trauma that's involved here, then it may take some time for him to come to terms with the new reality he now faces.'

'What do you mean by some time?' Liz asked.

Anders shrugged.

'It will be more like months than weeks I should think. For the past thirty years or more Martin has lived his life thinking that he knew everything about himself. Now it is as though the floor of his world has fallen in and below it another five years of life have rolled over him like a mental tsunami. It will take him some time for him to adjust.'

'But he will get better though?' Liz asked anxiously.

Anders flashed Alice a look. She shook her head very slightly.

'Yes he should get better, yes of course,' Anders said.

'You don't sound that convinced,' Liz said. 'Don't wrap me in cotton wool Anders. I need to know the truth, all of it.'

Anders flashed Alice another look. She pursed her lips before nodding her head.

'It's the residual guilt that worries me. The reason he forgot was because he blamed himself for his brother's death. It sounds crazy to us as he was only five years old at the time but he had it drilled into him when he was young by his mother. He was the eldest and it was his job to look after Eddie. Emotionally he may never be able to shake that guilt off.'

'So what might happen then?' Liz asked.

Alice took her hand in hers.

'Knowing Martin he will recover, he is young and strong,' Anders said. 'With help he'll be able to go back to work and pick up the threads of his life, in time that is.'

'There's a 'but' though isn't there? Isn't there?' Liz insisted with a rising voice.

'You may have to prepare yourself, Liz, he might not be the same person you married,' Anders said.

'But he will get better, eventually. Won't he?' Liz asked.

'I honestly don't know how well he'll deal with it all in the long run. I honestly think that there's a chance that he might never be the Martin you knew ever again.'

Chapter Twenty Four – Afterwards

They released Martin from hospital just over a week later. Even after all the tests they hadn't found anything physically wrong with him. Before he left the doctor made some appointments for him with the local psychiatric team that serviced the university. Liz turned up by herself to pick him up. She had decided that it might be better this way as it would give them a chance to talk as they drove home.

He was very quiet and so she tried to fill the silence on the way back with small talk. Martin just nodded at her and looked out of the window. She found it hard work and she was glad when she finally pulled up outside of their house.

Anders, Alice and Jerzy were waiting outside for him. He smiled a vague smile at them all and nodded but again he said very little.

'Come inside,' Liz said with a false cheerfulness.

They walked into the living room.

'Look, it's all actually tidy in here for once,' Liz said.

He glanced around the room and gave a nod of the head and another vague smile before he sat down in the armchair. This surprised Liz as he never normally used the armchair. He always used to sit on the sofa so that they could sit next to each other.

'Here let me take your jacket off,' Liz said with a smile.

Alice could see that her daughter in law was nearly in tears as she removed Martin's coat. He did little to help her, he just sat there like a young child.

'Come on Liz let's make a cup of tea for everyone,' Alice said brightly as she led Liz into the kitchen.

Liz just made it inside the door before she burst into tears.

'Oh Alice, where's Martin gone? Where's my husband gone?' she cried.

'Don't fret so dear,' Alice said as she held her. 'It'll take time, you'll need to be patient.'

Afterwards Jerzy described what happened to Lydia.

'God it was awful. Everyone was smiling, or trying to, and chattering away but he just sat there. You know what he reminded me of? Someone who was very old and very frail, you know what I mean? I don't know if there was anything of the old Martin there at all.'

Lydia gave Jerzy a hug.

'As everyone keeps saying it will take time.'

'Yes but how long?' Jerzy said. 'God I hate seeing him like that, he's like something out of 'The Walking Dead'. You know, when he does get better, do you think we should tell him?'

'I don't know,' Lydia replied. 'Let's wait and see how things go shall we?'

'Yes, we'll just wait and see.'

Jerzy waited for over six weeks before he started to see a glimmer of the old Martin once again. It was an extremely depressed and miserable version of the old Martin alright but it was at least something he recognised. He really felt sorry for Liz. She was losing weight with all the running around looking after him and she looked worn out.

Anders and Alice had rented a villa in Portugal for a few weeks and Liz and Martin had joined them there. Jerzy thought he looked somewhat better afterwards. He guessed that some long conversations with Anders might have helped.

It was a further three weeks before he turned up at work. He opened the door of the lab to see Jerzy reviewing the data from the Black Vaults on a large screen virtually second by second. Lydia was sitting next to him taking notes on a laptop.

'Has my assistant got an assistant now?' Martin asked with a smile.

'Prof, you're back!' Jerzy said with a big smile.

He jumped up and gave Martin a massive man hug.

'How are you doing?' Jerzy asked.

'Well okay until you nearly squeezed the life out of me. How are you Lydia?'

'I'm fine Professor,' she replied with a bright smile.

'I hear that you two are an item now,' Martin said. 'How are you finding it?'

'It's great,' Jerzy said, 'Well better than great actually. Lydia didn't like where she was living so she's moved in with me.'

'It's a lot quieter there, well most of the time,' she said with a cheeky smile as she looked up at Jerzy.

Martin looked at the two of them and thought that they somehow looked so right together.

'How's the analysis going?' Martin asked.

'Well it's going but it's a bit of a slog,' Jerzy said. 'There's just so much data and I don't want to miss anything. At least another seven or eight weeks I'd guess.'

'Well that's good but don't kill yourself. I still need to complete all the textual analysis of the notes and that's going to take some time too. I've been doing some of the work at home so I've already made some headway but it will still take some weeks to complete,' Martin said. 'Then there's the follow up interviews to do as well. I've scheduled those for early next week.'

'Glad to be back?' Jerzy asked.

'Yes I am. Work is what I need right now.'

And indeed Martin threw himself into it. Liz preferred this version of her husband to the near zombie that had come home from the hospital but she was still worried. All he did now was work and he was too intense about it. She kept hinting that he should pace himself but he didn't listen. She was scared that working too hard might lead to him having another breakdown.

The feared breakdown came but it had nothing to do with his working too hard.

He was in the lab catching up with Jerzy when he asked a question that had been bothering him for a while. He'd put off asking about it but he felt that he needed to know the answer sooner or later. He felt stronger than he had before and thought that he could take any new revelations.

'I just want to ask you something. I can remember everything that happened until I blacked out, at least I think I can, but did anything happen afterwards?'

'Afterwards?' Jerzy asked nervously.

Jerzy and Lydia exchanged glances after which neither of them could look Martin in the eye.

'Yes afterwards, after I blacked out.'

'Afterwards? No, I don't think so,' Jerzy replied as he still avoided any eye contact.

'Jerzy why don't we play poker?'

'Because you always win.'

'So what aren't you telling me?' Martin asked.

Jerzy looked at Lydia again and she shrugged her shoulders as an answer.

'Look I now know that something happened and I'm not going to give up until I find out what it is,' Martin persisted. 'So you might as well tell me. I'm okay now Jerzy, you don't need to swathe me in cotton wool.'

'Okay,' Jerzy said admitting defeat.

He opened a file on his laptop and ran it forward to a particular point. He played the soundtrack on the speakers.

'Eddie? Eddie is that you? Is that really you?' Martin heard himself ask.

'Martwen? I can't hear you Martwen.'

The child's voice sounded modulated, almost as though it had been synthesised, but it was definitely Eddie's voice. Martin had to exert some self-control to stop the tears from coming again.

'Eddie, I'm here Eddie. Can't you see me?'

'Martwen, is that you? It's dark here, it's dark here Martwen.'

There was a pause.

'Martwen! Martwen!'

Then there was a loud thump.

'That's you hitting the floor,' Jerzy said.

There was another pause then Eddie spoke again.

'See you soon, Martwen.'

Jerzy stopped the playback.

'That's it,' he said.

Martin was silent for a while as he absorbed the meaning of what he'd just heard.

'Don't tell Liz about this,' Martin said. 'Under any circumstances don't tell her.'

He made Jerzy and Lydia promise. He then nodded at them and shuffled out of the room without saying another word. He sat on a bench outside not seeing the grass or the sky or the students passing by. He could only think of what he'd just heard.

See you soon, his dead brother had said.

Martin knew that he'd just been handed a death sentence.

Chapter Twenty Five – A Breakdown

Martin felt incredibly tired again. As soon as he got home he went to bed. He stayed there for over a week. He didn't care if he ate or drank or lived or died. Liz was once again at the end of her tether but she calmed down when Anders told her that it wasn't uncommon for further breakdowns to happen and that they should lessen over time.

He awoke one morning and the sun was peeping into the bedroom through the centre of the curtains where they hadn't been pulled over enough. That shard of light shimmered as it hit the wall and it looked almost mystical to Martin. Liz was fast asleep beside him. He got up as quietly as he could and walked out of the bedroom into the living room. He pulled the curtains wide and he was bathed in golden sunlight and the reflection of the greenness of the garden outside.

He looked out and everything looked bright and new and strange to him. He took a chair outside and sat in the garden. It was a chilly morning but he didn't mind. Every blade of grass, every leaf on the trees and every bird singing away seemed like a miracle to him at that moment.

What is it? he asked himself.

It was life.

He'd been avoiding life since he'd heard Eddie's last words and this suddenly struck him as being very odd. If you only had a short time left to live then shouldn't you be making the most of it? Shouldn't you be living as if every day might be your last and packing in as much as you can?

He smiled to himself. Whatever the future had in store for him will happen and he had to accept that. He was certain that Eddie's words were true and he also knew that there was nothing he could to alter it.

Nothing except live.

Liz was worried when she woke up in an empty bed. She rushed into the living room and smelt the wonderful smell of bacon cooking. Martin was in the kitchen moving bacon about in the frying pan.

'Just thought I'd do something nice for breakfast,' he said.

He smiled at her. Not the vague smile or the 'I'm so sorry' smile of recent weeks. It was a real smile, a Martin smile. He was back.

She kissed him and held him close. She could feel that he was aroused by this and she suddenly wanted him, wanted him more than she could ever remember.

'We can eat later,' she said turning off the cooker.

She led him back into the bedroom and they made love. It was intense and needy and reminded Liz of when they'd first fallen for each other.

The change in Martin was commented on by everyone. It was like a switch had been pulled and the old Martin had been magically restored except that it was a Martin that had even more energy and purpose than before. He worked hard but he also spent more time with Liz, every second was precious to him now. They ate out more and went out on little trips every weekend. Martin wanted to leave some nice memories behind for his wife.

There was still a black cloud in his mind that hovered over everything he did or thought. A cloud made up of a feeling of guilt that he couldn't shed and a feeling of his impending doom. He worked on and tried to keep strong.

He finally got around to carrying out the follow up interviews. He started with Josh.

Josh
'From your notes it would seem that the only manifestation that you felt affected you personally was what we've called 'the 'pay-ma' manifestation which was pretty intense. Is that right?'

Josh was dressed as scruffily as ever and he'd even kept the Ghostbusters cap to wear to the interview. However he looked quite relaxed and happy to answer Martin's questions.

'Yes, I mean some of the other stuff was quite unsettling and that thing with the phone stands was outright scary but the 'pay-ma' manifestation as you call it, I really felt that.'

'Have you had any thoughts on why that might have been the case? Have you remembered anything since we had the sessions?' Martin asked.

'I haven't remembered anything as such but I did find out something that you might find interesting.'

'Go on.'

'I asked my mum if she could remember anything that happened to me when I was a child that might explain the way I'd felt. She did. When I was about two and a half I got pneumonia, it was bad enough that they had to take me into hospital.'

Martin remembered the feeling of being ill during the manifestation, it felt like flu but worse.

'Anyway they had to give me some injections and the first doctor who did it botched the job a bit and hurt me. I went into hysterics because of the pain. Afterwards anyone who came near me wearing a white coat would cause me to have hysterics again. Mum said it frightened her so much that she asked the doctors to take their coats off before coming in to see me. She also told me that they had to give me gas and air to sedate me before they could give me any more injections.'

'The visual manifestation was this big white blob. Could that be the white coat that scared you so much?' Martin asked feeling excited.

'Yes that's what I was thinking too. There's something else, I apparently invented a name for the doctor with the white coat. I called him the 'Pain Man'.'

'Pain man? Oh my God yes 'pay-ma'!'

'That's exactly how my mum told me I used to say it. I wasn't so good at speaking at that age.'

'Wow, that's so interesting,' Martin said feeling even more excited.

Josh gave Martin a shame faced look before he spoke again.

'There's something else that happened.'

'What?'

'During the 'pay-ma' manifestation, as you call it, I wet myself. I didn't tell you at the time because I was ashamed but I'm telling you now just so you know everything.'

'You wet yourself?' Martin said with a smile. 'That's so cool.'

'How is that cool?' Josh asked looking puzzled and not a little offended.

'Because I was absolutely sure that I'd wet myself too. Even after I checked my crotch and felt that it was dry I still had that feeling. So did Jerzy.'

Josh obviously didn't know what to make of this.

'So I not only wet myself but you and Jerzy felt it too?'

'Yes that's right.'

'Bloody hell that's so embarrassing.'

'Why?' Martin asked. 'We're all scientists and this is a really interesting piece of data. Anyway you shouldn't feel embarrassed. At the time it happened your body was being inhabited by a two and a half year old boy who knew that he was just about to be injected. I'd think the majority of us would have wet themselves in that situation.'

Josh gave this some thought.

'Yes I hadn't thought about it like that,' he said with a smile.

'So what did you think of the experiment in general?'

'Well in hindsight I just wish we'd all known exactly what we were letting ourselves in for but how could we? None of us, including you, had any real idea of what we were going to face. It was scary and unsettling and even mind-boggling at times but it was also important. You've started a whole new field of enquiry here, do you know that professor? What are you going to call it?'

'Call it?' Martin replied. 'My God, I'd not even thought about that.'

'Well you should,' Josh said. 'I think that this will be a field of study that many psychologists will want to get involved in, me for one. It would be nice if you could give it a name for when I specialise.'

After Josh had gone Martin sat there for a while letting Josh's last words sink in. He was right, it was a whole new field of study, a whole new 'thing' but he hadn't got the vaguest idea what he should call it.

He decided that he'd ask Jerzy and Lydia.

Madison and Jonathan

Martin had booked separate appointments for Madison and Jonathan so he was somewhat surprised to see them walking in together. He was also surprised to see that they were still holding hands.

'I was hoping to see you both separately, you know, for privacy,' Martin said.

'There would be no point,' they said.

They did that spooky talking in perfect unison again. Martin found this interesting straight away. Even with practice most people would need some sort of visual cue to tell them when to start talking so that they'd be in sync. Normally that cue would be a glance at each other's faces but Madison and Jonathan didn't do that. In fact they didn't look at each other once for feedback during the entire interview which Martin found quite staggering.

'Why wouldn't there be a point?' Martin asked.

'Something happened during the experiment, something profound...' Madison started.

'...and it's changed us. We're different now,' Jonathan said seamlessly completing the sentence.

'Okay,' Martin said looking closely at the two of them.

They looked normal, in fact both of them looked so much better than when he'd seen them last. Madison was dressed in a loose top and she was wearing loose fitting jeans and trainers. Martin had never seen her dressed so casually before. She looked calm and nowhere near as hyper as he remembered her as being. Jonathan was also dressed very casually and even slightly scruffily which was unusual for him too. Martin had been fairly sure that he used to iron his jeans before. His face looked different too, he seemed more relaxed and more open maybe. Their default expression seemed to be a smile.

'By the way we're sorry about the talking at the same time thing...' Jonathan said.

'...we're trying not to do that in normal circumstances as some of our friends find it a little strange,' Madison said.

'Okay,' Martin said as he looked at them with some uncertainty. 'Well before we go into that I'm interested in your take on the manifestations. I have to say that the most spectacular ones were when you were both together and it looks to me as if they might be related to particular events that happened to each of you. Would that be correct?'

'Yes the smashing of plates and walking on glass were to do with Maddie,' Jonathan said. 'That was her father you heard doing that. He was a violent man and he used to beat up Maddie's mum quite a lot. He used to swear at her and accuse her of sleeping with other men. Of course Maddie didn't know what he meant by this at the time as she was only four. When they argued Maddie used to get scared and hide away. There was a space behind the washing machine in the kitchen that she could just about squeeze into. While she was hiding she used to recite a rhyme...'

'Yes, 'Janey and Johnny sitting in a tree', wasn't it?' Martin said.

'That's right,' Jonathan continued. 'Her mother taught it to her, she said it was a song that she used to skip to with her friends when she was Maddie's age. That night, the night when all the plates were broken, was the night that Maddie's father murdered her mother.'

This made Martin sit up.

'My God, I'm sorry. If I'd have known that...'

'How could you?' Jonathan continued. 'Maddie couldn't really remember it herself. The voice you heard was her father's. He was looking for her and he would probably have killed her too if he'd found her. The police broke down the door the next day and found Madison's mum battered to death and her father hanging from the top of the stairs. She was only discovered later by accident when one of the forensics team heard her sneezing. After that she was brought up by her aunt and they never talked about her mother once. She tried to forget and she succeeded most of the time but the sadness and loneliness that she felt in that hiding place stayed with her. She tried to ignore it and that worked some of the time but, when she couldn't, she tried to numb her feelings with drink and sex. That didn't work either. She was basically a mess and she only volunteered for the experiment because she was going through a particularly bad patch and she thought it might take her mind off things.'

Again Martin noticed that the two of them hadn't exchanged a single glance. They weren't wrong when they said that they were different.

'As for Jonny,' Madison said, 'he was a little boy of six when his mother died from cancer. His father was overcome with grief and loneliness and he invited his older brother, Jonny's uncle, to stay with them. His father found Uncle Bob's presence comforting but Jonny didn't. Unfortunately for Jonny his uncle had a liking for little boys and, as he was the only one in the house, his life then consisted of a constant struggle to keep himself hidden away and to make sure that he and his uncle were never alone together. It didn't always work.'

'Was it the uncle who shouted the word 'Boy'?' Martin asked.

He expected Jonathan to reply but it was Madison who continued.

'Yes that's right and you can probably guess what Mr. Sausage was. Jonny used to say a prayer too when he was hiding...'

'Oh yes it was 'Safe, safe in the dark...' wasn't it?' Martin said.

'Yes that's right. Anyway, on top of grieving for his mother, poor Jonny had to put up with this situation for just over three years. He felt ashamed and dirty every time he got caught by his uncle but he couldn't tell his father. Even though he was just a little boy he knew it would break his heart. So he kept quiet. Then Uncle Bob died and Jonny was so happy. His happiness didn't last long though. He'd prayed for his uncle's death so many times but, when he saw his father's grief, he felt incredibly guilty and felt as if he'd murdered his uncle himself. He feared people after this and kept them at arm's length. He feared intimacy too and he was a virgin at the time of the experiment.'

Martin looked at the two of them again not quite believing what he'd just heard. They showed no emotions while they told each other's stories, indeed they both looked relaxed and even happy.

'You know so much about each other. I take it that you've talked about your childhoods a lot since the experiment?' Martin asked.

'No we've never spoken a word to each other about it...' Madison said.

'...not once,' Jonathan added.

'How is that possible?' Martin said feeling both confused and that he might be on the edge of something really important.

'The 'ghost field', as you've called it, had to open our minds to get at our deep childhood thoughts. Before you ask we have no idea what 'it' is just what it did to us,' Jonathan replied. 'While our minds were open they sort of touched and overlapped each other. I was fully aware of all of Maddie's thoughts...'

'...and I of Jonny's,' Madison continued. 'I knew not only what had happened to him but how he'd felt at the time. His memories became part of mine. But there was more...'

Without a pause Jonathan said, '...because not only were our memories shared but so were our feelings. After that last session I could feel Maddie's need to get out of the pub. She needed to go somewhere dark and become small so she would feel safe. I felt that need so...'

'...we went to bed and he held me,' Madison said. 'He told me that I was safe and for the first time in my life I actually felt that I was. That was because he told me not with words but with his feelings. Feelings don't lie. Then I felt his need. He needed sex but he was scared of it too. So we had sex and it was incredible...'

'Well you don't need to go into that,' Martin said feeling that he was intruding on something private.

'But I do,' Madison continued. 'We had sex but it was different. I could feel what Jonny was feeling, not just the need but the pleasure too...'

'While I could feel what Maddie was feeling. Afterwards I asked Maddie if it was always like that...'

'...and I told him it was never like that. It wasn't just the pleasure but how Jonny felt about me. He liked me, not just my body or my face but me. He knew everything about me and he still liked me. I wasn't prepared for that,' Madison said.

'So you felt some sort of empathic link after the session?' Martin asked hoping he'd picked the right words.

'Yes I suppose that might describe it but it's more than that...' Madison said.

'...we've become even closer since the time of the experiment,' Jonny said. 'While there's a person called Maddie and another person called Jonny we're not separate entities. We know what the other is feeling every second of the day. We know we love each other but we feel it will become even more than that in time.'

'How could it become more?' Martin asked feeling somewhat stunned by where all this was going.

'We're becoming one,' Madison said. 'We're getting closer every day, every minute, we can feel it. We're not like most couples who might doubt their partners at times, who fight, disagree and have misunderstandings. All of those things are impossible for us.'

'If you know everything about someone, and I mean everything, and you know how they're feeling then you know why they're feeling the way they are. There can be no doubts or misunderstandings because *you know*,' Jonathan explained.

'What did you mean by 'becoming one'? Martin asked.

'Do you ever ask yourself if you love yourself or fall out and have an argument with yourself or ask yourself how you're feeling?' Jonathan asked.

'No of course not, no-one does, unless they're a little weird I suppose.'

'We don't do that anymore either,' Madison said. 'We don't talk to each other when we're alone. Our thoughts are increasingly becoming shared, it's like the dialogue that you have with yourself while you're thinking. We're becoming one person with two bodies and it's entirely wonderful.'

Martin was speechless for a while. He'd thought that his discovery of the 'ghost field' had been important but it was nothing compared to this.

'What does it feel like?' he asked.

'We can't think of our former lives without feeling so sorry for those two lonely and desperate people. We aren't lonely anymore, we are loved and understood and respected. And we know it,' Madison said.

'It feels like I thought heaven would be,' Jonathan added.

After the interview Martin sat there for some time thinking about what he'd learnt. He knew that not only was it the most important thing he'd ever discovered, he thought that it was the most important thing that ever could be discovered. He felt as if he was looking at a possible future for the human race, a future where everyone knew and totally understood everyone else, a future without war and violence and greed and hate. It might possibly be the greatest advance in human history since the invention of tools and fire.

He'd asked if they would agree to take part in some further detailed research but they refused. They asked for what they'd told him to stay confidential as they had a life that needed to be lived. However they didn't rule out doing some research in the future. They did agree to take part in some informal interviews with just Martin present so long as he kept everything about them totally to himself.

He was totally stunned and had to force himself to focus. He still had one more interview to do.

Lydia
'In your notes the only manifestation that you felt was related to you personally was when you heard a bird in the room. Can you tell me about that and why you felt it had something to do with you?' Martin asked.

'I thought that I'd forgotten all about it but it seems that you can never really forget anything. Sitting in the darkness I started thinking about my mum and, when I heard the sound of the bird, I remembered something. I must have been eight or nine and, around that time, mum almost lived in the church and she made sure I went with her too. She used to say that 'She feared for my soul and the damnation to come.' A nice thing to say to a kid but, if I'm honest, I hadn't got a clue what she was on about. I'd learnt to just let her words wash over me if you know what I mean.'

Martin nodded.

'I was in church one day and bored stiff as only a nine year old can be when I saw this bird. It was a dove I think. It was just sitting there in the rafters with its head going from side to side as if it was looking for a way out. It was trapped in the church just as I felt I was. It then flew around the church, fluttering this way and that, desperately trying to get out and, I know this might sound silly, but I really thought that it might be my own soul trying to escape. Most of the windows in the church were stained glass but there was this one window which just had clear glass. The poor bird must have thought it was a way out as it flew straight into it, not once but several times until it finally fell to the floor. Someone picked the bird up and took it outside, I was sure it was dead. I used to dream about that bird sometimes when I was young.'

'Yet you say you'd forgotten all about it?' Martin asked.

'I certainly hadn't thought of it since mum died. If I'm honest I try not to think about her at all. It's just too painful.'

Everything he'd heard in the interviews seemed to fit in with his theory. Somehow the 'ghost field' stimulated these repressed and forgotten memories. As to how this happened Martin didn't have a clue. It might take a lifetime of hard work to find that one out. Martin sighed.

A lifetime was something that he just didn't have.

Chapter Twenty Six – A full circle

It took Martin just over six weeks to complete the textual analysis and, even with Lydia's considerable help, it took Jerzy a little more than that to finish the data work. Once this had been done they needed to try and integrate the two analyses and Martin was dreading this. However, it went better than he'd expected, mostly die to Lydia's input. She was fantastic at structuring things and between the three of them the paper started to take shape.

They were now working to a deadline as they had a space booked for publication in one of the better known psychology journals. They had nearly finished the paper when they finally came to the stumbling block of what to call 'it'. Between themselves they'd always simply called it the 'ghost field', imagining something like an electric field that enabled ghosts rather than the flow of electrons, and it had stuck. So they'd referred to it as that in the paper until they thought of a better term. When they couldn't think of anything else and, with time running out, they decided to just leave it as it was. And so the area of study that was to become known as the 'Jorgensen-Kowalski Ghost Field' was born.

Martin was as happy as he could be in the circumstances. He was working so hard that he didn't have time to think of much else. However something happened just before publication of the paper that forced him to think again about the future.

He'd come home late one evening to find Liz seated at the dining room table. She had a strange look on her face. A stab of fear immediately pieced Martin's heart. He had the thought that she was going to tell him that she'd had enough and she was leaving him. After all he'd put her through he wouldn't have blamed her. This had been his secret fear for some time now and he desperately didn't want to lose her.

'Can you sit down please Martin?' she asked. 'I've got something to tell you.'

The 'please' was strange too. She never said 'please' to him, unless she was angry that is. He sat down next to her and attempted a smile. He looked at her face but he couldn't tell much from her expression.

'I'm sorry Liz, I know I've been working too much lately but...'

'It's not about that,' she said. 'I know how important your work is and how important it is to you.'

'Then what?' he asked.

'I'm afraid that I'm going to tell you something that will change both our lives.'

'Go on,' Martin said as he girded his loins for whatever Liz was going to say.

'I never thought it would, or indeed could, ever happen but it has. Martin I'm pregnant.'

'You're what?' Martin said in absolute astonishment.

He had to ask because he was almost certain he was going to hear the words 'I'm leaving' and wasn't sure that he'd heard properly.

'I'm pregnant,' Liz said in a nervous voice.

'That's what I thought you'd said but then I thought I must have heard it wrong. My God, you're expecting! When?'

'I'm seven weeks gone,' she replied. 'I knew a couple of days ago when I tested myself but I just couldn't believe it. I didn't want to say anything to you until I saw the doctor and he confirmed it. What do you think?'

'What do I think?'

In truth Martin's mind was in a complete whirl.

'I mean are you happy about it?' Liz asked.

'Happy? No that wouldn't cover it, I'm absolutely ecstatic about it actually!'

And he was. They had been trying for a child for so long that he'd almost forgotten why. The desperate aching need for a child had been hidden away like so many things that couldn't be coped with. He also knew that he'd be leaving something of himself behind after he was gone. Liz wouldn't be alone and that was a massive relief too.

They hugged and cried and finally remembered to call their parents and share the good news.

Martin's first child, as Jerzy had jokingly started to call it, was published a few weeks later. They knew that the paper was revolutionary and that it would probably be quite controversial too. They waited for the fallout with some trepidation. However in the days afterwards they heard exactly nothing and Martin didn't know whether to be disappointed or relieved. As time went by he was coming down firmly on the side of disappointment.

However Liz's bump was getting bigger and Martin started throwing himself into everything baby related that he could. He attended every antenatal class and appointment with Liz and proudly shared the picture of the ultrasound scan with anyone who would let him. He practised every exercise with Liz and together they planned the birth down to the finest detail.

While all this was going on Martin received an invitation to speak at one of the big psychology conferences. They wanted him to present his paper and talk about the 'Ghost Field'. Martin accepted straight away but as the day drew nearer he began to wonder if it had been such a good idea.

Liz and Jerzy and Lydia went with him. They met Martin's parents at the conference. He suddenly had some suspicions.

'Is this all something to do with you?' Martin asked his father.

'No, not at all,' Anders replied. 'One of the organisers, a friend of mine, approached me to ask if you'd be interested and I said that you might. Apparently they've been getting quite a lot of contacts about your paper.'

'Really? I thought that no-one had read it.'

'Well I think you're about to be surprised,' Anders said.

The seminar was packed and there wasn't even any standing room left when Martin started speaking. The presentation itself went well but the question and answer session afterwards became quite intense. To Martin's surprise he received quite a bit of support from some delegates. The detailed evidence had persuaded them that it was at least worth looking into. However there were more than a few sceptics who were willing to dismiss the whole idea out of hand. Martin was a bit put out about this until his mum pointed out that, whether they agreed with it or not, they were all talking about it.

The presentation got mentioned in one of the broadsheets and after that it all went totally crazy. Martin got a shock one morning when he walked past his local newsagents and one of the tabloids on display had the headline 'Eggheads prove that ghosts are real!' He bought a copy and read it. He turned to the story on page four only to see a big picture of himself. Of course they'd garbled and simplified the whole thing but the important fact was that they were talking about it too.

After that the talk shows wanted interviews with him and, because he looked quite young and could string a few words together, he became quite popular. At around this time the pub, now totally refurbished, was about to open again and they invited him and Jerzy along.

Martin was quite curious to see what they'd done with it and, anyway, a free pint or two with Jerzy sounded like a good idea so he took them up on their offer.

It was still called The Black Vaults and, while the outside of the pub and the pub sign looked familiar, the interior had been totally transformed. They'd done it out to look exactly like it had at the turn of the century except for the fact that it was all themed around ghosts. Martin thought that it looked a little like an extension of the London Dungeon. Wall plaques gave information about the gory events that were supposed to have happened within the pub walls and there were also lots of plaques about the experiment and the newly discovered 'Ghost Field'. Most of the plaques seemed to be perpetuating the garbled version of events that had been spread by the tabloids but Martin wasn't really surprised by that.

Amidst all of the back slapping, hand shaking and photo opportunities he managed to get a moment to himself upstairs. A spiral staircase now led up from the bar downstairs. It wasn't a room anymore it was a 'mezzanine restaurant'. The bottom third of the room, where they'd sat during the experiment, was now just fresh air and he could look down on the bar below. Lining the walls on either side of him stood rows of tables and chairs, ready and waiting for hungry customers. He walked down towards the bottom of the room where a column of blue light shone down from the ceiling just in the place where the cold spot had been.

He stopped and placed his hand under the blue light. It wasn't cold but warm. He looked around and found it hard to believe that the experiment had really happened right on this spot.

Not long after that came the book. A publisher had offered him and Jerzy a sizeable contract to write a popular book about the experiment. They got permission to include about some of the things that had happened to Josh, Madison and Jonathan and then they got writing.

One good thing that also happened around this time was that the university, finally acknowledging the attention that Martin and Jerzy's efforts had brought to the university, appointed Jerzy as Assistant Professor with quite a reasonable salary. Martin was delighted about this as he'd already picked Jerzy out in his mind to be his successor. It would be one less thing to worry about.

Although Liz was heavily pregnant she helped Martin and Jerzy with the grammar and punctuation while Lydia made sure that the structure and chapters of the book worked properly. Liz was eight months gone when the book was published. 'The Ghost Field' went straight to number one on both sides of the Atlantic.

A month later Liz gave birth.

All of the careful plans they'd made went straight out of the window when Liz's waters broke unexpectedly. Martin lost his way when driving to the hospital even though he'd driven there at least twenty times before. The labour took a long time and, in the end, the doctors decided that they needed to cut Liz to get the baby out. Martin got gowned up and went into the theatre with her, hoping that he'd get to hold her hand while the surgeon did what he needed to do further down.

'Not cutting the cord?' the surgeon asked him.

Martin had forgotten all about that.

'Yes, yes of course,' Martin replied.

'Well you'd better get down this end then,' the surgeon said with an amused smile.

Martin watched with morbid fascination. He could see the top of his child's head but that was all. A lot of preparation and then a quick cut and it seemed like the baby flew out. With a shaking hand he snipped the umbilical cord using a weirdly shaped pair of scissors. A team of two whipped the baby away and checked it over before wrapping it in a blanket. They sat Martin down and then handed him the bundle.

'Here's your son Mr. Jorgensen,' the doctor said.

Martin looked at the squidged up features of the scrap of life he'd just been handed. He looked like a cross old man. His son! He suddenly felt such love for the child that it filled him up and he started crying. He and Liz had made this and he knew that his life would never be the same again.

And it wasn't.

When thinking about it later he always marvelled at the fact that two of them had gone into the hospital but three of them had come out. He would spent time just looking at his son and wondering about the miracle that had brought him to them.

In all this the dark cloud was still there, in the background maybe, but Martin never doubted Eddie's words for a moment. He took out as much insurance on himself as he could and resigned himself to his fate. Luckily the money was flowing in from the book and the TV appearances so Liz would be okay and she'd always have Eddie to comfort her.

It had been Liz's idea. After he'd been born they had discussed several names but Liz was firm. Her favourite grandfather had also been called Edward so why not? Martin kissed her and gave in. He'd never loved her more.

Eddie, as he quickly and inevitably became known, started growing up and gaining his own little personality. Martin watched this both as a father and professionally and found it fascinating on both levels.

Life was good for Martin but the dark cloud in the background never went away.

Eddie was nearly three when Martin came home one evening. He'd come back from a book signing for his and Jerzy's latest book, the follow up to 'The Ghost Field', and it was around eight in the evening. When he got back Liz was asleep on the sofa. At the other end Eddie was also fast asleep with his head on a cushion and a blanket wrapped around him.

Martin smiled at the two sleepers and then he carefully picked up his son. He held him so that his little head lay on his shoulder. His son's arms automatically went up around his neck. Taking his son to bed was one of Martin's favourite duties. He laid him gently down on his bed, tucked him in and turned on the nightlight. His little head lay on the pillow with his half-clenched hands on either side. Martin found his teddy bear and tucked it under the duvet before kissing Eddie's forehead. He stood for a while and just looked at his beautiful son before tip-toeing out of the room.

He turned off the light switch and softly said, 'Nighty-night Eddie.'

He turned to go but then his son said something in a sleepy voice.

'Nighty-night Martwen.'

Martin stood motionless as if turned to stone. He played back what his son had just said over and over in his head. When he could finally move he turned around and Eddie was just as he had been, fast asleep. He sat by his son and looked on him in wonder.

He now knew what Eddie had meant when he said 'See you soon.'

The tears started flowing. For the first time since the experiment the dark cloud of guilt and fear evaporated and he felt light and free. While the tears he cried might have been partly tears of relief, he knew that they were mostly tears of gratitude.

He felt grateful that he lived in such a magical universe as this one for, although it was vast and its machinations were infinite, it had somehow conspired to bestow the greatest gift that he, or any human being, could possibly have wished for.

A second chance.

Two Years Later

She looked at her watch and started mopping even harder. She was a little behind schedule and it was important that she got off on time today. It was Saturday and she'd promised to drive her daughter and her friends to the shopping mall. Ines knew that she'd been looking forward to this for weeks and she didn't want to disappoint her.

She stopped mopping and smiled. Children these days expected so much. When Ines had been young she'd lived in a dusty remote village in Portugal that only had three shops and there was nothing remotely attractive about any of them.

Well the world changes, she thought.

She looked again at her watch, she was doing well. She'd finished the downstairs bar and toilets so she only had the restaurant upstairs to do so she should have plenty of time. She emptied the dirty water out of her mop bucket and refilled it. She walked past the spiral staircase to the small lift that people in wheelchairs used to get up to the restaurant. There was no way she was going to carry such a heavy bucket up the stairs.

As soon as she got upstairs she started mopping away but, after just a few minutes, she became aware of a strange sensation. She felt a prickling in her head and the hairs on the back of her neck started standing up. She felt as if something was about to happen, although what that might be she had no idea.

A noise made her look towards the bottom of the restaurant. There was nothing there, just the blue light at the end of the room but it looked different now for some reason. She looked at it closely and was amazed to see little blue lights start to peel off it and circle around it at speed. They were like little blue fireflies.

A feeling of fear began to build up inside her. It was somehow familiar but she couldn't think why. Then she smelt a combination of rank body odour, piss and cheap wine and this triggered something in her mind. She heard a door slamming and it made her jump. The fireflies were spinning ever faster around the blue light.

'Ines!' a voice called. 'Where's my dinner?'

'No, no it can't be,' she said to herself.

'You lazy little whore, where's my dinner?' the voice shouted angrily.

She remembered.

She thought of her grandfather for the first time in many years. When she'd been a child she'd been sent to live with him after her grandmother had died. He was a violent man, especially when drunk, and she'd quickly learnt to keep out of his way or she'd have to face his fists and his boots.

'Mary Mother of God, no you can't be here, you're dead,' she whispered as she crossed herself several times.

A figure stepped out of the blue light, a black shape in the outline of a man. Its blackness had depth as though she was staring through the figure into a space beyond. The figure turned and looked straight at her. It was still all black except for the fact that it now wore her grandfather's face!

She screamed and ran towards the stairs. In her haste she knocked over the mop bucket but she didn't care. She ran straight out of the pub and into the street. She stood there shaking for a few minutes before she started to calm down. She rang her daughter first and told her that she was on her way home. She then rang her boss and handed in her immediate notice.

Meanwhile upstairs the water had fanned out slowly over the restaurant's floor. It ran down towards the far end of the room, towards the blue light. Shortly after this the residual flow had to go around something, a circular object had formed on the floor and it was illuminated by the blue light above. It was white and sparkled in the light as if it had been coated with diamonds.

It was a perfectly round disc of crystalline ice.

Shadows appeared within the blue light, flickering and moving as if blown by some unseen wind. The blue light suddenly failed, its hot bulb shattered as the fingers of icy cold finally penetrated its protective case. Without the light the shadows could not be seen but they were still there.

Waiting.

The End

I hope you enjoyed this story. If you have please leave a review and let me know what you think. *PCW*

You can find out more about me and my books here
-
https://patrickcwalshauthor.wordpress.com

Made in the USA
Monee, IL
14 March 2023